A secret rendezvous . . .

I fished inside my blouse and took a note out of my bra.

"What on earth is that and why are you keeping it there?" Bella asked.

"Because it's precious and it's private. It's from Simon."

Bella read it.

"Gadzooks, sirrah," she giggled, "an assignation! How smashing! Wednesday at five . . . uhm . . . I think I'm just going to creep up to the Tower Room and . . ."

"Don't you dare, Bella," I shouted. "Oh, you wouldn't, would you? Oh, please, please don't spoil it."

"'Course I won't. Never let it be said that Bella Lavanne stopped the course of true love running smooth . . ."

I sighed. "But look at the note. Don't you think it's blissful?"

"I don't know that I'd necessarily call 'Dear Megan, How about Wednesday at five, Tower Room? Love, Simon,' *blissful* . . ."

THE TOWER ROOM

THE
TOWER
ROOM

ADÈLE GERAS

Harcourt, Inc.

ORLANDO AUSTIN NEW YORK
SAN DIEGO TORONTO LONDON

Requests for permission to make copies of any part of the work
should be mailed to the following address:
Permissions Department, Harcourt, Inc.,
6277 Sea Harbor Drive, Orlando, Florida 32887-6777.

www.HarcourtBooks.com

First published in Great Britain in 1990
by Hamish Hamilton Ltd.

First U.S. edition 1992

First Harcourt paperback edition 1998

The Library of Congress has cataloged an earlier edition as follows:
Geras, Adèle.
The tower room/Adèle Geras.
p. cm.
Summary: Living at the secluded girls' school where her foster
mother is headmistress, Megan falls in love for the first time, with
the young man the foster mother has chosen for herself.
1. Schools—Fiction. 2. Love—Fiction.
3. Foster parents—Fiction.
I. Title.
PZ7.G29354To 1992
[Fic]—dc20   90-19530
ISBN-13: 978-0152-05537-0 pb   ISBN-10: 0-15-205537-1 pb

Text set in Janson Text

A C E G H F D B

Printed in the United States of America

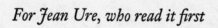

For Jean Ure, who read it first

En la noche dichosa
En secreto, que nadie me veía
Ni yo miraba cosa,
Sin otra luz y guía
Sino la que en el corazón ardía.

Upon that lucky night
In secrecy, inscrutable to sight,
I went without discerning
And with no other light
Except for that which in my heart was burning.

FROM *Saint John of the Cross: Poems*
TRANSLATED BY ROY CAMPBELL

Up in the tower, nothing seemed real
except the sky, and you, at night, calling.

FROM *Letter from Rapunzel* BY FRANCES WILSON

THE TOWER ROOM

Once upon a time, the linoleum was green. I remember it clearly from my first day at Egerton Hall. I was not quite eleven then, and of a fanciful turn of mind, and I imagined it as a ribbon, streaming down the three stories of Austen House, snaking all along the corridors and winding around the stairwell, slipping down over the stairs and along Study Passage until it met the brown linoleum that marked the beginning of School Corridor. Of course, it's not like a ribbon at all, and it isn't even properly green anymore. All those shoes: regulation lace-ups, Sunday-best brown ankle-straps, the Staff's Cuban heels, muddy lacrosse boots, grass-stained tennis shoes, and, more recently, Saturday night Sixth Form stilettos (officially forbidden but still worn) have left their mark. The lino is cracked, pocked, and scuffed and looks pallid from the attentions of a thousand mops.

LONDON *APRIL 6, 1962*

There it is: a beginning, and exactly the way a beginning ought to be. Once upon a time. I miss Bella and Alice. I miss the Tower Room, even though we're high up here as well. I am alone almost all the time, and these words are company. It's my eighteenth birthday today and I've hardly noticed it. I told you about it, of course, and tonight we will go to the pictures to celebrate, but there are no cards from Bella or Alice or any of my friends, and nothing from Dorothy. I will send them all this address today, just to let them know where we are. I want to be seen to be behaving responsibly. I can't decide what to do, what ought to happen now, but I feel that if I write the whole story down, try to analyze it all in a way that even Dorothy would approve of, then everything will become clearer. I hope it does, and more than that, I hope that you read this one day, because in all this time, we've never spo-

ken very much, or if we have, then they
haven't been the right words.

I came to Egerton Hall for the first time in
January 1955, just over seven years ago. My
father had already left for Africa, and I used to
enjoy imagining him in a jungle surrounded
by heaps of bananas, with monkeys swinging
from creeper to creeper around his head.
We'd driven from the station in a taxi, my
mother and I. It was five o'clock and snowing
heavily. Fat flakes broke against the windshield and drifted and blew outside the cab
like ghosts. Up and up the drive we went, and
as we turned into the gravel courtyard in front
of Main School, I caught sight of a huge building, even darker than the dark sky, with rows
and rows of lighted windows set into the
black. Like topazes lying on black velvet,
that's what I said then. What a peculiar child I
must have been, but even now I can recall how
comforting it was to see that yellow shining
out in the night. The whole place looked mag-
ical to me, like a castle in a toy snowstorm, the
kind you pick up and shake so that the flakes
will fly about. What else can I remember? My
mother's face, very pale, both of us trying hard

not to cry, and Dorothy standing beside a polished table that seemed to stretch for miles and miles. Dorothy waiting to receive me.

I had been hearing about Dorothy since infancy. She was a friend of my parents and particularly of my mother. I didn't know her age exactly, but she must have been in her late thirties when I first arrived at Egerton Hall. She had been our neighbor long ago. My mother loved to walk in Dorothy's beautiful garden. She often told me of how generous Dorothy was with the abundant produce of her vegetable patch. During the time my mother was pregnant with me, it was Dorothy who gave her the asparagus for which she had a craving. Shortly after my birth, however, Dorothy had taken up her teaching post at Egerton Hall, and, since then, my mother had spoken of entrusting me to her care.

"Dorothy will see you're properly educated," she used to say, or, "You'll be well looked after with Dorothy," and now here she was, just as I'd seen her in my parents' photograph albums: small and gray-haired (had she always had gray hair, even in her twenties?) with startling light blue eyes, dressed in a suit of greenish tweed.

"Hello, Dorothy," I said.

"Welcome to Egerton Hall," she answered, almost but not quite smiling at me.

After my mother had gone, I tried imagining her in the fantasy jungle with my father, but it was hard. For a long time after that night, when I thought of her, I thought of her face in the taxi's back window, a small, ivory shape, disappearing into the snow and out of sight.

I never saw her or my father ever again. They died that spring on a trip upriver, and Dorothy adopted me legally. It was a very straightforward matter. She was already my guardian while my parents were abroad. I can hardly remember my sadness now, but the feeling I had of being completely alone in the world was very strong. No brothers, no sisters, no aunts or cousins, only Dorothy, and no home apart from a small room at Egerton Hall. Everything I possessed was capable of being packed into my school trunk. For a while after my parents died, I used to dream at night of places in Africa and Asia where I had lived with them when I was a very young child. I dreamed so much that what I actually remembered about each place became blurred and misty and all the different scenery ran together in my mind, and soon all that was left to me was an unfocused image of somewhere full of sunshine and blue water and very green trees heavy with purple, scarlet, crimson, and vermilion flowers.

"Welcome, child," Dorothy said to me that first night. "As soon as you're ready, we'll walk across to Junior House and find your dormitory. I want you to regard Egerton Hall as your home as well as your school."

Which of course it was, until a few weeks ago.

LONDON *April 7, 1962*

It's difficult to know how far back to go. I think I shall start just before the beginning of last term, the last day of the Christmas holidays, and if I have to refer to things that happened further back than that, then I can do it as I go along.

"Be sure that what you write, that *everything* you write, is relevant, germane to the issue." Oh, I can hear you saying it, Miss Doolittle, and I'll try. I will try.

The Christmas holidays were nearly over. I liked Egerton Hall with no one in it. Of course, I missed Bella and Alice, missed the laughter and the noise and even quite looked forward to lessons, but there was something especially quiet and more than a little eerie about a building that was accustomed to being full of people and loud with voices, and that found itself, all of a sudden, empty. It seemed to me sometimes as I walked along the corridors during the holidays, listening to the squeak of my own shoes, that everything was holding its breath, waiting for something. Desks looked at me as I passed, lockers in the cloakroom hung open expecting shoes, pianos in the practice rooms hummed quietly under closed lids, and curtains hung at windows, looking out. I decided to go and have a look at the Tower Room before everyone arrived. I hadn't been up there since returning from my visit to Alice's house, where I always spent a part of the holidays.

The Tower Room was the highest room of all, right at the top of Austen House, and the only room with three beds in it. It had sloping ceilings and a large window that looked down over the front drive and the fountain in front of Main School. From it you could see past the sweep of lawn that stretched to the lacrosse fields, and beyond those, to the trees. Even more important, from the Tower Room window you could get an uninterrupted view of the sky, and living there, I became a sky-watcher in the same way that other people become bird-watchers. It didn't matter to me what the weather was like. I loved the massed, bruise-colored clouds of a storm and the little cotton wool puffs of early spring. I admired the high blue dome of summer and the low gray ceiling of rainy November. Best of all, I liked the way the light left the sky after a day full of sunshine: bleeding out of it slowly before the darkness came.

Bella, Alice, and I regarded the Tower Room as ours.

"But Sixth Formers have never shared a three-room before," Miss Herbert, the House-mistress of Austen House, had said when we'd been to see her at the end of the Fifth Form. "You'll all be House Prefects next term, you know. Besides, you've had the Tower Room for a year and perhaps there are others who would like it. I'm sure you'd all get used to single rooms ... and anyway, your A-levels will be coming up soon ... hours of private study ..." On and on she had gone, but we (mostly Bella, it was true) had wheedled, cajoled, and persuaded, pointing out how the rest of the House could be accommodated in single, double, and four-bed rooms, saying that everyone knew ours was the only three-some, etc., etc. In the end, Miss Herbert had given in. She was a thin, dark woman with her hair bobbed ("Just as it must have been in the twenties," Bella used to sigh. "Desperately unfashionable!"), and she had the face of a well-bred and quite pretty horse. Her clothes tended toward the brown, and her shoes Bella regarded as unspeakable: thick-heeled, high-laced clodhoppers. Still, she had long fingers, which Alice said were aristocratic-looking, and I admired her exquisite jewelry—a magnificent amethyst brooch pinned to her tweedy lapel and a half-hoop of opals the size of small peas on the fourth finger of her right hand.

"It's not bad luck for her," Alice had said when she saw it. "Her birthday's in October, so it's her birthstone." Alice is the sort of person who knows about such things. Miss Herbert taught Latin and I liked to think, during weary translations from Cicero, about who it was who had placed the opals on her hand. Perhaps it had been intended as an engagement ring, and Miss Herbert's fiancé had been tragically killed during the Second World War, and since that day Miss Herbert had stopped thinking about men at all, but had devoted herself instead to looking after the girls of Austen House.

"You can tell from her ornaments and things that she has taste," Alice used to say. "I'd love to see her house. It must be very elegant and refined. Not a bit like Miss Doolittle's." Miss Doolittle was Assistant Housemistress. She taught English and lived in a room of spectacular chaos. She looked like nothing so much as the figurehead on a galleon: golden-haired, with slightly protruding eyes and an enormous swelling bosom that curved in front of her as she walked. She favored tight dresses of mauve crepe with draperies about the hips and high-heeled shoes of black patent leather.

"You can tell how plump she is," Alice said once. "Have you ever heard the deafening noise of her nylons rubbing together as she walks?" We collapsed into giggles on the candlewick counterpanes of the Tower Room.

I looked around at the empty white walls cleared of pinups, the white-painted chairs, chests of drawers, cupboards, and the beige squares of carpet material pretending to be warm, comforting rugs beside each of the beds.

At the end of the Fifth Form, Miss Herbert

had said: "Of course, if you have the Tower Room as Sixth Formers, I shall trust you not to abuse the privilege."

Bella had looked innocent, Alice really didn't know what she was talking about, and I answered for all of us, "We'll be very sensible about talking late and so forth. Really we will."

So it was settled. The Tower Room had been ours for two years and one term, and the three of us were still in it.

"The really good thing about this place," Bella used to say, leaning too far out of the window, "is the view. And the fact that it's up so many stairs that no member of staff is going to be bothered coming up here, are they?"

"Hope not, for your sake," Alice answered. "Do you truly like those horrible cigarettes or do you only pretend?"

Bella stopped leaning out of the window and turned to laugh at Alice.

"Oh, I love them, Alice . . . You're such a goody-goody at heart."

"I'm not a goody-goody at all. I just don't like the smell. It's awful. The taste's horrid as well. I had one at a dance once and I was practically sick."

"Just make sure you don't get caught," I

said. "I don't trust some of those Third Formers out there."

"They'd never dare tell on me, would they?" Bella's eyes looked very dark in her face. "And anyway, I'm careful as anything." And she was careful, in a reckless sort of way. She'd found a wonderful hiding place for her cigarettes and matches under the floorboards of one of the cupboards, hidden by about a foot of tangled games equipment: shorts, boots, balls, rackets, and lacrosse sticks. No one would ever look there, and (I supposed) one cigarette smoked after lights-out every few days couldn't really be considered wicked.

"There are girls out there of our age," Bella said once, waving her hand in the general direction of the outside world, "who are married with children. We are not kids anymore. We are almost eighteen years old. That's grown-up."

"I'd hate to be married at eighteen," Alice said, wrinkling her nose.

Bella laughed. "And we all know why that is, don't we, eh?"

Alice's eyes filled with tears. "Don't be so beastly, Bella. I told you and Megan all that in deadly secret. You don't have to tease me about it. I can't help it."

Alice's deadly secret (one the three of us had discussed long and vigorously under the sloping ceilings of the Tower Room) was that, as she put it, she was not "all that keen on kissing boys." She admitted to us that she had never yet met one boy who made her heart beat faster, and she used to listen with wide eyes while others (well, mostly Bella, in all honesty) regaled her with tales of openmouthed kissing, fumblings with brassieres in the backseats of various cars, and, once, some nervous fingers on an upper thigh, above a stocking top.

"I promise you," Bella said, "nearly fainting wasn't in it. I can't tell you how delicious it felt. Waves of warmth sort of rushing over you."

Alice was unimpressed. She told me one day when Bella was in the bath, "I think she makes up half that stuff just to annoy me. I think she gets most of it out of books. Remember *Lady Chatterley's Lover* last year? How she carried it around covered in brown paper? It was all she ever talked about. I could never get into it myself."

I agreed with Alice about *Lady Chatterley's Lover*, but Bella and I had agreed between the two of us that Alice was definitely afraid of sex.

"I regard it as my mission in life to find Alice a boy she *will* be excited by," Bella used to say, and I'd answer, "How, stuck away in Egerton Hall with three hundred girls and an almost completely female staff?"

"Love will find a way," Bella would mutter mysteriously.

"You sound like a book," I'd say, and laugh.

I remembered that conversation now as I walked over to the window. The beginning of January, and no snow. The sky was whitish gray and there was no color anywhere. The whole landscape had taken on the appearance of a photograph. There were two magpies on the chimneys of Eliot House, and my heart lifted. Two for joy. I was superstitious about these birds, which seem, in their coloring and shape, almost too dramatic to be quite real. Their cry is like the noise of a mechanical toy, and one magpie, so they say, brings sorrow. If I ever saw a solitary magpie, I would scan the heavens for a long time looking for another, and if I couldn't find one, I would salute the bird and say, "Magpie, magpie, where is your mate?" to ward off harm.

Many birds liked Egerton Hall, and so did I. It was built in the shape of an *E* with one extra prong, or a comb with four evenly spaced teeth. I knew its history backward. In the eighteenth century, an enterprising and newly rich Egerton had built the hall in acres of expensively landscaped garden, and it is to be hoped that whoever had laid out the plan was not turning in his grave over the lacrosse fields, tennis courts, netball courts, open-air swimming pool, and other such monstrosities that had been added much later. There was still the terrace, and the fountain in the middle of the courtyard with its statue of nymphs and sea snakes intermingled so that you couldn't really tell where the ladies ended and their fishy friends began. There were still lawns and a kitchen garden, and there was the San, where we were sent when we were ill. A house had been built for the younger girls near what we called "The Rim of the Known World."

After that, there was the forest.

"Jolly clever of old Egerton to put his house here," Bella had said, long ago. "Think how useful for nature ramblers, botany freaks, mushroom collectors, etc."

"It's romantic," said Alice, thinking of "Babes in the Wood," "Robin and Marian," and other well-known tales of that kind.

"It's not a frightfully foresty forest, though, is it? More like a large wood. And a bit too near civilization to be wild or anything," I said.

Bella had snorted loudly. "I don't call Egerton Parva civilization and I'm not altogether sure that Coleston counts either, for all that it's a town and a famous eighteenth-century watering place or whatever."

Foresty or not, I thought, looking at the tops of black branches just visible behind the Chapel, there have been stories. I suppose it's natural for children to make things up. Once there was a rumor about an escaped lunatic hiding in there, then there was the time when Josephine Graham ran away and wasn't found for ages.... There had been a very strong "the forest has got her" gang at work then, but in the end she was discovered behind the bar at the pub in Egerton Magna. Still, whichever way you look at it, there's something strange about trees, and especially so many trees together. They do so often seem as though they are nearly alive, and it's easy to imagine that they are about to move, or have only just stopped moving, or even (like in the story of Daphne, who was forced to turn herself into a bay tree to avoid Apollo's lustful embraces) that the bark is a covering for some kind of body.

The nineteenth-century Egerton sisters, Phoebe and Louisa, inspired by Miss Buss and Miss Beale of Cheltenham Ladies College and Miss Lawrence of Roedean School, decided an educational establishment was just the ticket, and proceeded to organize one the moment their father was safely dead. They had no tiresome husbands to put down feet in the way nineteenth-century husbands were wont to do, and so they had a grand time remodeling Egerton Hall. Apart from defacing the grounds with various sporting facilities, they built a chapel (all white marble and Victorian stained glass) and had the stables converted into an art studio, decorated with Art Nouveau tiles of lilies in bronze and eau-de-nil and murky pinks and mauves. They installed a science laboratory and called each "wing" of the original building a House, naming them after famous women writers: Eliot, Austen, Brontë, Browning. Each House has a long passage called Study Passage where the prefects' studies are to be found, three floors of bedrooms and bathrooms in assorted shapes and sizes, a Junior Common Room (J.C.R.) complete with phonograph, small fiction library, and copies of the *Daily Telegraph*, *Punch*, and the *Illustrated London News*, and a Senior Common

Room (S.C.R.) for senior girls who are not prefects. The younger girls do their prep in the J.P.R. (Junior Preparation Room) with a prefect to supervise them, but Fifth and Sixth Formers are left to their own devices in the S.C.R. A great deal of toasting of crumpets by the gas fire goes on, and much reading of novels and writing of letters. Each House also has its own dining room and kitchen. Miss Herbert has three well-appointed rooms to herself: a drawing room, a study, and a bedroom. Miss Doolittle has a drawing room and a bedroom. Then there's Matron's Room, like a cross between a hospital and a nursery in an old-fashioned children's book, full of cupboards packed with Virol, bandages, iodine, Friars' Balsam, packets of sanitary napkins, an impressive array of pills and potions, and a phalanx of fearsome silver instruments of a medical nature.

The Egerton sisters had clearly been of the opinion that luxury was wasted on the young, and so the girls' rooms are uniformly spartan. We have candlewick counterpanes in shades of pink, blue, yellow, or lilac, and curtains with a flower pattern made almost invisible by countless washes, and that's that. Everything else is added by whoever's living in the room:

posters, books, photographs of parents, or pets, or (later) boyfriends, and ornaments of all descriptions. There are crazes for things. I remember an especially disgusting statuette of a cat I had, which was supposed to turn blue when it rained and pink when it was fine. Everybody had one at this particular time except (typically) Alice.

"I can see what the weather's like just by looking out of the window," she'd said. "And besides, they're hideous, those things."

She wrinkled her nose. It was remarks like that, made in the calmest and gentlest of voices, that gave Alice a reputation for taste and refinement and earned her the nickname of "Princess Alice."

"That," Bella used to remark, "and the fact that you live in the palace next door."

"It's not a palace!" Alice always rose to the bait. "Only a biggish house. And I don't call five miles away next door, either."

"Biggish!" Bella would roll about and clutch her sides. "Fifteen bedrooms—biggish! Listen to her!"

"It's not my fault," said Alice. "It's where I was born. And you don't live in a hovel either, so there, Bella Lavanne!"

"Keep your hair on." Bella smiled. "You're

a very nice, kind princess, and we don't care at all how rich and grand you are. We forgive you."

"I'm not grand!" Alice would start to wail again, and I'd end up throwing a cushion at her.

I sat in the Tower Room and wished that the holidays were over and that it was tomorrow already, and then they'd be back. During the time I'd spent staying with Alice, gales had blown away much of the roof of Austen House, and now there was scaffolding around most of the brickwork that faced the main courtyard. This cat's-cradle of metal pipes came right up to the window of the Tower Room, and in places there were planks balanced between one bar and another, so that the men (who were, it seems, replacing the whole roof bit by bit) could walk about comfortably.

Dorothy had said, "Of course, it will take the whole term to complete the work."

"Surely not!" I answered. "There must be a whole crowd of them, isn't there?"

"Yes, of course, but they can only work after you girls are safely in lessons, and, naturally, they have to finish before it gets dark. We don't want any nonsense about the men looking at the girls in their bedrooms. As it is,

Miss Herbert will have to warn all of you to be particularly vigilant about putting away your pajamas in pajama cases, or neatly under the pillow, and not leaving your belongings lying about your rooms."

Stockings drying on a towel hung over the towel rack, a few hair rollers left out on the chest of drawers, fluffy slippers peeping out from under the bed: I imagined these things driving the poor workmen into frenzies of unrequited lust, so that they plummeted off the scaffolding and down to the gravel below. Bella would be sure to try to talk to them. Alice would be nervous. . . . They'd be so rough. It would all be immensely interesting.

I went to look out of the window, and there, suddenly, was Dorothy, looking up at the Tower Room. It's freezing, I thought, but still, I'd better, just the same. I opened the window.

"Hello, Dorothy!" I called.

"Hello, dear," said Dorothy, craning her neck. "You look extremely . . . medieval."

"I'm jolly cold."

"Then close the window and come down. We'll have some tea. I've a piece of news you may find interesting." Dorothy smiled and waved and strode off toward Brontë House, where she had a small flat, being not only

Head of Science, but also a kind of caretaker as well. As always, it seemed to me that, Cheshire catlike, a faint impression of her smile hung in the air after she had gone. I shook my head to get some sense into it. As I closed the window, I noticed that my hair, which I wear in one long plait down my back, was wet at the ends from brushing against the windowsill.

LONDON *April 9, 1962*

We were lucky to find this place. It's a studio apartment near Gloucester Road tube station. It's very high up, on the fourth floor, but I, at least, am used to that after the Tower Room. We've tried to make it as nice as possible, but, as you often tell me, we haven't got much money to spend on posters and things and I didn't have a chance to bring much with me. A letter came today from Miss Herbert. She must have asked Bella or Alice for the address and written at once. She says:

> I would ask you to consider most seriously, Megan, what you are in danger of losing. All the efforts of the last seven years (yours and your teachers') will come to nothing if you persist in the path you have chosen. At least keep the work going in case you do return to

Egerton Hall. You know, of course, that there have been voices raised in favor of your expulsion, but Miss Donnelly, Miss Doolittle, Miss Clarke, and I have carried the day, I think, and should you decide to come back, I'm sure it could be arranged.

I have brought my books. I read them all the time when I'm not writing, and not doing my shift at the coffee shop. I can't believe my friends and I ever thought that being able to work for a few miserable pounds a week was glamorous. I think I was very spoiled at Egerton Hall, even in the matter of views from the windows. Here, there are red-brick houses in every direction as far as the eye can see, and the people look like insects, so far below me that I cannot make out their faces at all. The sky at night is a kind of mucky gold because of all the streetlights, and during the day it resembles old dishwater, but perhaps that's only my mood. There are some sunny days, from time to time.

In Dorothy's room, I drank my tea in silence. Silence was one of the things I'd had to get used to since my parents had died. Dorothy only spoke when it was necessary to do so, and then as economically as possible. I filled in the time that hung between one sentence and another by looking at the room and at Dorothy in it. There was something cool about her. I decided that it wasn't just the pale blue walls of her sitting room, nor the bone china teacups that were so white they seemed luminous, like ice. It was Dorothy herself who made everywhere she went less warm. It was hard to know her age, and she never referred to it, but the iron-gray helmet of hair had remained unchanged for as long as I could remember, and above the fireplace there was a photograph of her in a gown and mortarboard at her degree ceremony, which showed the same pale eyes and the same sharp features that I had known most of my life. There was only one picture in the room: a view of mountains capped with snow, and even the armchairs had straight backs. Good posture was something Dorothy believed in, along with economy of speech, hard work, early rising, and prose. She had never said so directly, but I knew Dorothy felt there was something soft and squashy and not quite correct about poetry, because it often dealt with feelings and emotions and these were squashy, soft, and not quite correct, either. Or perhaps it was

only my poetry she didn't approve of. . . .
She'd never have dared to speak out against
Keats or Byron or Shelley. That would have
been Philistine. Still, I knew Dorothy's opinion of "adolescent scribblings."

"They are usually," she had said once, "a
morass of sentiment and couched in words
that are of the most violent purple imagin-
able."

I didn't argue. One didn't lightly bandy
words with Dorothy. I had been fourteen at
the time, and I vowed then and there never
to show Dorothy another poem of mine, not
ever.

She was clearly in no hurry to break the
silence. I thought about words and came to
the conclusion that that was why I liked them
so much: because Dorothy was so stingy with
them. Azure . . . translucent . . . iridescent . . .
viola . . . antique . . . they're like jewels, I
thought, all different colors. I liked taking
them all out and arranging them this way and
that, and putting them in lines and making
patterns with them . . . ineffable . . . scarlet . . .
peonies . . . wine . . . leaf . . . japonica . . . gar-
denia . . . camellia.

"Are you," said Dorothy, "feeling confident
about the examinations?"

I put my cup down, feeling irritated suddenly by her maddening behavior. No one else would invite you to hear an interesting piece of news and then not tell you . . . but the rituals had to be reenacted over and over again.

"Yes, I think so," I replied. "Of course, I shall have to study all next week."

"Of course."

"But I think I've got it mostly under control."

"Excellent." Dorothy continued taking small bites from an apparently never-ending biscuit, and said at last, "I have a somewhat unusual item of news. I only heard finally today . . . ," she paused and looked at me. "I have found a replacement for Miss Bristow." Her eyes shone and a small, enigmatic smile touched the corners of her mouth.

"That's good," I said. "You must be very relieved."

Privately I thought: Why is Dorothy finding a new laboratory assistant so exciting? Miss Bristow had left suddenly last term, no one quite knew why, although naturally there had been rumors. There were always rumors.

"A young man called Simon Findlay is arriving tomorrow to help us out. Only a temporary appointment, I'm afraid, as I believe he has other plans for next term, but still, it will be a help to me."

Dorothy leaned forward to put her cup back on the tray. Young probably means thirty-five, I reflected, but it was best to be sure.

"How old is Mr. Findlay, exactly?" I asked.

"He's twenty-two," said Dorothy. "I do hope some of our more frivolous girls can be persuaded to curb any silliness."

I took a biscuit from the plate. I could hardly ask how handsome he was. Dorothy would definitely class that as "silliness." In any case, I thought, I hardly ever go near the labs, and so will probably see very little of him. I decided to stop thinking about him, although of course Dorothy was right, and there was almost bound to be "silliness." In her magic kingdom of silver instruments, glass beakers, and vials of unnaturally blue and red and yellow crystals, where white light shone down on luminous and nonluminous flames of Bunsen burners, where everything was capable of measurement, analysis, and description, such things as the feelings of one person for another were out of place and incomprehensible. The younger girls were often "keen on" one of the prefects, although so far I had escaped such adoration. Bella and Alice had their share of admirers, though, who brought them bars of chocolate after they'd been out with their parents, sent them sloppy cards for their birthdays, and watched them hungrily in chapel, on the games field, or in the dining hall.

"There's nothing sexual about it," said Bella once, last year, in the cloakroom of all places. Bella was the expert on such matters. "It's simply that everyone needs someone to love and admire and these kids pick the nearest and most glamorous creature they can. If it can't be Elvis or somebody, it's got to be someone near at hand."

Alice smiled. "Are you saying you're glamorous, then?"

"The most glamorous thing you've ever seen," said Bella, and she started to do a belly dance in her netball shorts and gym shoes.

"Bella, they're waiting for you on the court," Miss Robbins called out, and that was the end of that conversation. I recalled it now and thought: This new young scientist chap will probably fall for Bella. Or perhaps he's engaged.

"I'm sure most of us," I said, "have too

much work to do to trouble our heads with young men."

Ten out of ten! That was precisely the sentence Dorothy had been waiting for. She rewarded me with one of her rare and beautiful smiles and rose to her feet.

"Good girl, Megan," she said. "He is a very talented young scientist, far too talented for such a relatively menial position. I wonder whether I might not entrust him with some teaching... only the lower forms, of course..." Her voice slid away into silence and she became lost in her thoughts for a moment. Then she gave an uncharacteristic laugh, almost as though what she'd been thinking about had embarrassed her. It seemed to me that she was blushing, but perhaps she was only feeling warm. She stood up and went over to the window.

"I know I can rely on you." She pulled the curtains across. "How very early the dark comes down at this time of year, doesn't it?"

"Yes," I said. "Yes, it does." I stood up, too. "I should go now, Dorothy. I'd like to go and see Miss van der Leyden. I'm sure she must have arrived by now."

"By all means, dear," said Dorothy. "I have

some work to do before supper. I shall see you at half past six."

Miss van der Leyden still lived in her little room right at the top of Junior House. I could have gone straight up the stairs, but I never did. Every time I visited her, I made a point of walking through the dormitories. Blue and Green, Violet and Rose were the biggest, and as I strode along the narrow strip of appropriately colored carpet, I glanced in at the quiet cubicles and remembered all the sounds: the giggles and whispers, the squeaks and crashes, and often, especially on the first night of term, the sounds of homesickness—muffled sobs and sniffs and the padding of slippered feet from those who had undertaken the task of cheering people up. I couldn't remember crying much. I paused at the cubicle nearest the door in Violet, which used to be Bella's, went in, and sat on the bed. I tried to look into the mirror that stood on the chest of drawers but had to bend my head right down.

"I can't ever have been this little," I said aloud, and my voice rang through the empty space, and the mauve curtain that formed a kind of flimsy front door for the cubicle stirred slightly.

Bella had been as nosy then as she was now. I remembered the conversation perfectly. It was more of an interrogation than a conversation, but I hadn't minded. Bella was so beautiful. I had stared and stared at her, and thought: Her hair is so black, it's almost blue . . . and her skin. . . .

"Hello," Bella had said. "Come in. Isn't this a funny place? I haven't really got used to it yet, even though I've been here for a term already. It isn't a bit like I imagined. Have you read the *Malory Towers* books? I have. They're super. I'd hoped we'd have midnight feasts and things, but we didn't last term. I'm Isabella Lavanne, but you can call me Bella. What's your name?"

"Megan Thomas."

"Why have you only come in January? Everybody else came in September. Oh, except for someone called Alice Gregson. She's new this term, too. I think she's in the cubie next to yours. Yours is over there. Look!"

"Cubie?" I was lost already.

"Short for cubicle," said Bella, "which is what this teeny-weeny little bit of space with wooden partitions all around it is called."

Bella had evidently forgotten all about her question. Why had I only come to Egerton

Hall in January? I really had no idea at all. Perhaps it was something to do with my eleventh birthday. Maybe you could only come in the term during which you had your birthday. I would ask my mother in my first letter home. I thought with pleasure of my red zip-up writing case, complete with a little book of stamps. There was a compartment for the air-letter cards I had to use to write to my parents, but I couldn't imagine who I was going to write to on the pad of azure Basildon Bond. Bella interrupted my daydream.

"Where do you live?"

"I live here."

"No, silly. I mean where do you live in the holidays?"

"Here."

This had silenced Bella for about five seconds, but then she'd said, "Why?"

My parents were still alive then. I said, "Because my father works abroad, and my mother's gone to be with him, and there aren't many schools where they are . . ."

"Who will look after you?"

"My guardian."

"What's a guardian?"

"Someone who looks after you when your parents aren't there. My guardian is the

Chemistry teacher in the Upper School. She's called Miss Dorothy Marshall."

"My mother's dead." Bella put a picture in a leather frame on the chest of drawers next to a china pig decorated with pink flowers. "That's her."

"She was very pretty."

"Yes, she was. My stepmother's quite pretty, too, but not as pretty as my mother. My mother wanted me so much, and then she died while she was having me."

"That's sad." I had had trouble keeping back the tears that sprang to my eyes.

"I don't feel especially sad about it. What I mean is, it was ages and ages ago, so please don't cry."

Bella was taking handfuls of clothes from her trunk and pushing them into the drawers. "Actually, I think it's rather romantic. Like something in a story. Have you got any brothers or sisters?"

"No," I said. "Have you?"

"No, but I wish I did have. Sometimes I think I should make up a brother and pretend to have him. I don't see how they'd find out, do you? Shall we do that? Yes, let's . . . Go on, it'll be our secret."

I laughed into the silence, recalling the

Danny episode. Bella had invented a brother so plausibly that everyone believed her for ages, and it was only when Miss Baker, the Housemistress of Junior House, had asked Bella's father how his son was that the story fell to pieces.

I left Violet and went upstairs to Blue and Green. Walking through them, I thought of Mack, who had been Matron then. Miss van der Leyden had only been Under Matron, second-in-command in those days to Miss McLaren, who was an elderly, thin, sandy-beige person with "a shortbread look about her" as Alice had once put it, and an iron will. Mack would stride through the dorms on sheet-changing days calling out, "Top to bottom and bottom away!" which sounded vaguely nautical, like "Avast the mizzen mast!" or whatever it was that sailors shouted from the rigging. Miss van der Leyden would clump along behind her, reminding us to change our knicker linings and collecting all the laundry bags to put in the big wicker basket outside on the landing. I thought: I wonder if the Juniors still wear knicker linings or if they call them knickers now? Maybe those heavy-duty navy bloomers we all wore over our ordinary white knickers are a thing of the past . . . and do the poor little Juniors still have to wear those horrible, scratchy, knee-length socks made of wool?

"What I want more than anything else in the world," Bella used to say in those days of Liberty bodices and elastic suspenders for keeping the dreaded socks up, "is a garter belt and some stockings. We can wear them on Sundays when we're in the Upper School. I shall have American Tan stockings and a lace brassiere."

Bella had been the first to wear a garter belt and stockings and now she's the first to wear tights . . . always racing ahead, Bella was, rushing into things. Unlike Alice, who never saw any good reason for change, and was nearly fifteen before she went into stockings, and then only did so because of Bella's constant nagging.

At last, I reached Miss van der Leyden's door and knocked.

"*Ah, ma petite fleur!*" cried Miss van der Leyden as soon as the door was open, and she hobbled over to enfold me in her arms. I closed my eyes and let the fragrance of mint, face powder, and rose-geranium toilet water wash over me. Miss van der Leyden's smell was the smell of childhood, of safety, of home.

For the first time that day, I felt warm. I sank down into a small armchair beside the gas fire and looked around at this room that I liked almost better than any other at Egerton Hall.

"I love your room," I said. "There's so much to look at. I love all the photos, and knickknacks and bits of wool, and the cushions and the lovely china with blue pictures on it . . . oh, I love it all."

"It is, how do you say, 'a filthy mess,'" said Miss van der Leyden, "but it is my home."

"Really? Do you think of it as home? What about Belgium?"

"No, no, *chérie*, I have told you many times before. From there I am . . . what is it you say? Exiled."

"But you don't have to be. No one exiled you, did they? No one said you couldn't live there, did they? You could go back, couldn't you?"

"But there is nothing to go back for. I have been here so long."

"What about your family, though? Don't you miss them?"

"Well, I still see them, of course. I visit. But they all have lives, concerns of their own. Also, I am not a relation of whom one would boast,

n'est-ce pas? Like you girls say: the ugly mug!"
Miss van der Leyden's laughter filled the small
room.

It was undeniable. Miss van der Leyden is
the ugliest person I have ever met. Long years
ago we had all called her "Quasimodo" and
speculated late into the night about the causes
of such ugliness. Celia Hammond, who read
spy stories, thought she was a foreign agent.
Mary Gillis thought she was a witch, and at
first no one could look her straight in the eye.
The fact that she was Belgian and spoke English with a strange accent did not help. But it
didn't take long for us to grasp the main fact
about Miss van der Leyden. She loved us. We
were her children. Oh, the other staff were
dutiful and caring and conscientious all right,
but Miss van der Leyden loved us. Mack
would slap the plaster on a cut knee, and Miss
van der Leyden would hug us and cuddle us
and give us a surreptitious sweet. If you were
sick in the night, she would sit with you and
sing to you and hold your head over the basin
and clean you up beautifully afterward. If you
were homesick, she would take you up to her
room and show you photographs of Belgium
and tell you stories about her childhood, about

her grandmother teaching her to make lace, oh, about all kinds of things. She was a mother to us and better than a mother: completely uncritical and undemanding. Provided you kept your cubicle tidy, that was good enough for her.

I said, "Do you remember how you taught us knitting?"

"Agony!" said Miss van der Leyden. "That is what it was. Oh, I was in despair sometimes with you. How clumsy you were! And how dirty the wool became . . . and how you could never count properly and above all how you did not grasp the—how do you say—the principles of knitting."

"But you had Alice, didn't you?"

"*La petite princesse!* The little angel! Now she . . . she was dainty, and careful, and so neat. Do you remember how she used to embroider those tray cloths printed with flowers?"

"She still does embroidery and tapestry and knitting. Most people think she's mad."

"Mad? Because she is not jumping to the Elvis music and sitting in cafés her whole life? Ah no, she is not mad at all. She is above all that."

"But what's she going to do when she leaves?" I asked. "She can't sit in a room and embroider all day. She's going to have to go into the world, isn't she?"

"So are you all, *chérie*," said Miss van der Leyden. "So are you all. You will have a cup of coffee?"

"No, thanks. I've just had tea with Dorothy."

"I will have coffee alone, then."

As she busied herself with cups and jugs and spoons, I began to think about Alice.

Of all the people I have ever met, it is Alice who always seems to me vulnerable. The very first time I saw her she was crying. It was our first night in Egerton Hall, and after lights out I soon became aware of sniffing and weeping from the cubicle (cubie) next door. That's the other new girl, I thought first, and then: Why aren't I crying? I felt strange, and I think also a little sad, but I was somehow frozen. It was as though I knew that crying was going to be of no help. Perhaps I had some kind of premonition that this was going to be the only place I would see for years and years. Anyway, I was dry-eyed, and the misery I could hear next door distracted me still further from my own feelings. I got out of bed and went to see if I could help. Bella was already there, sitting on the bed with one arm around someone who looked, even in the dim light from the landing and with her nose bubbling and her eyes streaming with tears, like a princess from a book of fairy tales. Her hair fell in an undulating cascade down her back until it touched the pillow, where it lay spread out and shining in waves of reddish gold. I had never seen hair like that in my whole life, and it was all I could do not to put out my hand and touch it.

"This is Megan," Bella whispered. "Alice, look. Megan's new today, too, and she's not crying."

Alice held out her hand as if she were being introduced to someone at a garden party. I noticed how frail her arm was, and how I could almost feel each separate bone in her hand as I squeezed it.

"Cheer up," I said, somewhat inadequately. "Bella and I will look after you."

Bella nodded vigorously but corrected me nevertheless.

"I'll look after you both, Megan. Show you where to go and what to do. Everything. We'll be friends," she decided, and perhaps it was the firm way that she said it that made it so, from the first. Ever since that night, we have been friends, but our relationship has always had at its heart the shielding of Alice from the harshness of life. At times, over the years, I've been jealous when Alice has been nicer to Bella, or when I've thought she has, and I'm sure Bella is sometimes secretly peeved that I spend so much time staying with Alice during the holidays.

I've realized, also, that the way other people treat you has a great deal to do with how you look. I, for example, am tall and fair and placid-looking. In the mirror I see what I regard as a moon face and a long plait of hair that I call "dirty yellow" and Bella, kindly, calls "corn-colored."

"You look," she's often said to me, "like a Scandinavian milkmaid."

I think she means it as a compliment. I do not look like the kind of person others will rush to protect or cherish, like Alice, nor do I look exotic, flamboyant, and faintly dangerous, like Bella. What I look is strong and healthy and calm and reliable.

Miss van der Leyden's coffee was ready.

"How is Dorothy?" she said. "Did she have . . . did you both have a pleasant holiday?"

"We're fine. She's got a new lab assistant. A

young man of twenty-two called Simon Findlay. He's coming tomorrow."

Miss van der Leyden began laughing. She laughed so much she had to put her cup down and wipe her eyes with a lace-edged handkerchief.

"*Oh, là, là,*" she cried. "*Que ça va être amusant!*"

"What?" I asked. "What's going to be so '*amusant*' as you call it?"

Miss van der Leyden sniffed and the laughter subsided gradually.

"*Mais, figure-toi,* Megan, all you young ladies . . . your parents, they pay the money, much money, to remove you from the real world to here, a little fantasy world where there is only girls and more girls and lessons in things you can find only in books, and where you are far, far away from life . . . and now, look what happens. A young man will come from the outside, and he will be a cat among the doves."

"Pigeons . . . a cat among the pigeons."

"Pigeons, doves, what does it matter? You know what I mean."

"You mean, we're all going to go soppy over him. What Dorothy calls 'silliness.' "

"*Précisément.* Only, silliness I do not call it. I call it *tout à fait naturel.* If a young woman is locked away, as you are locked away, at the top of a tower for years and years ... imagine what can happen."

"I'm not locked away. I can go whenever I like. And I do go. Look. I spent a week at Alice's during the holidays, and I'm going to university next year."

"But you are still ... how do you want to say it? Removed from life. You know nothing, in spite of having read so much and in so many languages. You should try to guard it, this ignorance."

"But I'm *not* ignorant!" I was indignant. "I know all about things ... poverty, unhappiness, hunger. I read the newspapers. I know what's happening."

"But love," Miss van der Leyden said. "Do you know about love?"

"No," I said, biting back a rude remark that I'd been ready to make about Miss van der Leyden's looks not leading her to many experiences in that direction.

"You think," the ugly face smiled at me, "that I know nothing about such matters, with my beauty, no? But you will be surprised if I tell you, and this proves what I am saying: you know nothing of the world outside. Nothing of real life."

I saw a chance to direct the conversation on to a more interesting topic.

"Tell me about your love life, then . . . Go on, you've never told me. I'd love to hear."

"Perhaps another time. Now, I wish to hear all about your time with Alice."

So I started to tell her.

I never slept well the night before term started. Most of the time during the holidays I forgot about what Egerton Hall was like when it was full of people. It was almost as though it were quite a separate place from its holiday self, linked only by a similar geography. But the night before last term began, I felt restless and ill at ease. It was as though I were an actress in a play—some huge production with a cast of thousands—and I'd arrived early for that night's performance, and no one else was in the theater at all. I was waiting for the others to appear, put on their costumes, and take up their roles. I was waiting, too, to be myself, my school self, which differed from my home self by much more than a uniform put on and discarded. At home, alone with Dorothy, I

think I would have described myself as intro-
spective, shy, hardworking, and alone. When
the others arrived, all my friends, but especially Bella and Alice, I seemed to change
quite dramatically. For one thing, I talked.
Not quite as much as Bella, it's true, but then
there were few who could match her torrents
and waterfalls of speech. For another, I
became steady and reliable, one of Miss Herbert's right-hand girls. I was efficient and
good at seeing to things like the composition
of the Table List each fortnight, making sure
that sworn enemies weren't sitting next to one
another, and that prefects took turns to have
at their tables girls whose table manners were
enough to put you off your apple pie. Alice,
for example, had firm preferences when it
came to her table:

"I'm not having Joanna Burton and that's
that," she told me. "Have you ever looked at
the front of her tunic? All egg stains and spots
of marmalade."

She shuddered delicately, and I promised
her I'd do my best. After all, she had had me to
stay so many times during the holidays that I
owed her more than one favor.

I loved staying with Alice. Quite apart from
the luxury of "the castle next door" as Bella

called it, there was the great advantage of Alice's family.

Alice, like myself and Bella, was an only child, but she did have the A.A. "The Assembly of Aunts" (not Alcoholics Anonymous or the Automobile Association) was our name for the simply enormous Gregson tribe, although we also called them "The Flower Fairies of the Forest" sometimes, because all their names were either flowers or plants of some kind.

"However did you escape?" Bella used to ask Alice.

"I expect they ran out of garden names in the end. I mean, after thirteen of them . . ."

"It's very unimaginative of them," Bella said. "They could have called you Magnolia or Japonica or Tulip or something. Not to mention things like Poppy."

I made all the names into a rhyme, partly because I like doing things like that and partly to help us remember them all. It went like this:

> Rose and Lily, Marguerite,
> Petunia, Daphne, Myrtle sweet,
> Fleur and Marigold and May
> and we're not finished yet.
> There's Ivy, Hortense, Daisy,
> and the dreaded Violette!

"Why 'dreaded Violette'?" asked Bella, when I first showed it to her. "I mean, I know it needs something there for the rhythm, but why not 'lovely Violette'?"

"Because I don't think she *is* lovely," I said. "Alice says she's the black sheep of the family. And she lives in France."

"And what kind of flower, pray, is a Hortense?"

"It's the French for hydrangea, I think."

Bella sighed. "It sounds just like a gardening catalog to me. Poor old Alice!"

Alice's mother and father were wonderful people to stay with because we hardly ever saw them. They were much older than most parents. Alice's mother's hair was quite white and she made no effort to disguise it. Her father spent much of his time in the garden, communing with his roses. Roses grew everywhere on Mr. Gregson's land: he had beds of them laid out in formal patterns, he had bushes of them lining the drive. Every available wall had a rose trained to grow up it, and he had small trellises and arbors here and there in the grounds that you could walk in and the roses would meet over your head. Of course, the Gregson garden was not at its most spectacular in December.

"But wait till June, my dear," Mr. Gregson

said to me at dinner one night. "Wait for the night of Alice's eighteenth birthday party. That"—he winked at me—"will be something to see."

"As a matter of fact, I like it like this," Alice told me as we trod the chilly gravel paths, "only don't tell my father. I like the black branches and the thorns. You can see them so clearly when it's winter. In the summer you forget, and the leaves cover them up and all the flowers puff out so you never see them, but they *are* there all the same." Alice paused. "I like to see the thorns. Look how sharp they are!" She bounced the tip of a finger on one to show me. "They can really hurt, you know. You do have to take care how you touch the roses. That's the best thing about them: how dangerous they are without looking dangerous. I love that."

LONDON *April 10, 1962*

Who do I know here? Mr. Scarpetti, my boss. Patsy and Janey, the other waitresses on my shift. Miss Hills, my neighbor downstairs, and Mr. Steele, my neighbor across the passage, but these last only to say "good morning" to. The lady in the tobacconist's, the man in the grocer's, the ticket collector on the tube, the milkman—all these I just nod and smile at, unless I'm actually buying something from them. I'm alone in this room for most of the day, and then after my early evening shift at work, we two are alone all through the night. In one of the most densely populated cities in the world, why do I feel as though I'm in a desert?

At school, I had circles of friends: that was how I imagined it. Bella and Alice and I were like a stone thrown into a pool. There were a few people in a small circle around us, then a bigger circle after that, and still another. Bosom friends, friends, people you were quite friendly with, the rest of your class, the other people in your House, the rest of the school. And the teachers: I must not forget the teachers. They took the place of my parents, and Dorothy more than anyone. I suppose she must have loved me in her own peculiar way. I wonder whether she will ever be able to forgive me?

Bella arrived on the school coach with all the shrieking Third Years and Fourth Years. I was waiting on the terrace outside

Austen House and saw her waving frantically out of the window. She was talking, calling over the heads of the younger girls almost before the doors of the coach were opened.

"Marjorie made me come down on the train, can you imagine? With all the hoi polloi and positively no one to talk to. Oh, Megan, how lovely to see you . . . Come on, let's run away to the Tower. Is Alice here? Are there tons of duties we have to do?"

"Hearts and Lungs, Fleas and Lice, Weights and Measures," I answered. "The usual stuff. But let's go and put your case in the Tower Room first. Alice never arrives till later. I don't think she enjoys supervising all those queues of people being checked by the doctor and weighed, and as for Fleas and Lice . . . you know Alice. She'd be afraid of some kind of contamination."

"I do see her point." Bella panted up the stairs behind me. "It's all frightfully undignified—all that standing around in dressing gowns being checked. We've only just been done. I can't think why once a year couldn't be enough. Oh, blissful Tower Room!"

Bella sank on to her bed and looked as though she might stay there for the rest of the afternoon. I went over to the window and looked out.

"I say," I said. "Look at this."

"Don't tell me," Bella said. "You say it every single term: doesn't everyone look small, just like a crowd of beetles, so on and so forth."

"No, Bella, it isn't that . . . look . . . it's a man."

Bella bounded off the bed. "A man?" She adopted her African Explorer tones. "Good Lord, Frobisher, I thought they were extinct . . . are you ebbsolutely sure?"

"Yes, I am, and I also know who it is."

Bella peered out of the window. "Is that him? He looks a bit weedy to me. Very thin and what a long scarf he's got on." She leaned out as far as she could and started to wave. "Hardly Marlon Brando, is he? I mean, he's wearing glasses, of all things."

I said, "He's more refined than Marlon Brando. More intellectual-looking. The Dirk Bogarde type. I can't think why you're waving if you think he's so awful."

"Beggars," (Bella went on waving) "can't be choosers. He is of the opposite sex, and moreover he is here, in the purlieus of Egerton

Hall. Look, he's seen me. I think he's coming over here."

"Oh, gosh, Bella, whatever have you done? What if someone sees you? A member of staff?"

"They're busy checking people's heights and weights and things. Did you say you know who he is?"

"He's the new lab assistant. His name is Simon Findlay. He's twenty-two. Dorothy told me."

I leaned out of the window and looked down with Bella. The young man was standing at the bottom of the scaffolding, looking up.

"Hello," he said. "Can you tell me how I get to the Science Block? My name's Simon Findlay."

I could see Bella's Number Two smile (open and welcoming) spreading over her face.

"I'll be down in two minutes," she called. "If you want to wait there, I'll take you over. My name's Bella, by the way."

"Thanks," Simon shouted. Bella had flown out of the room. She'd left the door open, and I could hear her clattering down the stairs. He remained looking up and said:

"What's your name?"

"It's Megan. Megan Thomas."

Then a dreadful silence fell. He stood at the bottom of the scaffolding, staring up at me. He was very like Dirk Bogarde, only thinner, younger, and with hair that wasn't quite so dark. Even behind his glasses, I could see how blue his eyes were. I didn't dare move away from the window and besides, I didn't want to. I just wanted to stay there, looking at him. Then Bella appeared and started chatting away. This seemed to break the spell.

He said, "I expect I shall see you about," and waved up at the Tower Room window as he was dragged away. It looked to me as though Bella had actually put a hand on his arm to guide him. I didn't know how she could touch him, just like that. I would never have dared. After they'd gone, I sat on the bed. The room seemed altered. It was as though seeing Simon Findlay's face at the bottom of the scaffolding had shaken pieces in a kaleidoscope, so that all the individual physical features of the landscape, the room, the known universe, had been changed in some way I didn't at all understand. Or perhaps (and this is hindsight, of course) the world remained the same and it was *I* who was different. That, in any case, was the beginning. I didn't feel like going down and supervising queues. I didn't feel like checking that the Third Years were unpacking their trunks tidily. I took out the private notebook where I wrote my poems and wrote this:

I am in the window
and you've turned,
looked up to see
the frame around my face.

You are too far down
and leaving. Walking
toward the fountain
where the fish spring
silver from the nymphs'
encircling arms.

I am still waiting,
a portrait of myself
in the frame of the window.

If this was falling in love, it seemed too quick to me. I thought and thought about it. I was surprised and a little shocked at myself. Was it allowed, this strength of feeling, simply because I had looked at a person? I knew nothing about him. He might turn out to be boring, or unkind, or stupid . . . and somehow none of this seemed to matter. I wanted to be near him, with him forever. Perhaps I was not normal. Perhaps being on my own such a lot had addled my brain. I waited for Bella to come back with every separate part of me vibrating, like violin strings under the sweep of a bow.

We—Alice, Bella, and I—always talked for a long time after lights-out. As we were prefects and the ones in charge of ringing bells to tell everyone else when it was time to go to sleep, Miss Herbert assumed that at half past ten we would, naturally, turn our own light out without any need of supervision. And turn it off we usually did, not because we were especially obedient, but because it was such fun to lie there chatting in the dark, with the square of the window letting in the dim glow of the lamps along the drive, and a thin, yellow line of light shining under the door from the passage outside.

It's much easier to talk frankly in the dark. You can say things that you would never dare to say in the daylight, even to your very best friend. Any blushing that went on was unseen. You could even let the odd tear slide out of the corner of your eye and onto your pillow, although Bella had a kind of sixth sense about that and could always tell when one of us was miserable, however we tried to inject courage into our voices.

Lying in bed at night we spoke about everything. We analyzed everyone, from the Headmistress (a glamorous widow called Mrs. Castelton, whom we rarely saw except on ceremonial occasions) down to the annoying little pipsqueak of a Second Former who'd given Alice some cheek. We discussed food. We worried about exams. We put together any information we had about the private lives of members of staff and considered long into the night the probable effects of a new hairstyle or a new pair of shoes. We mourned the fact that we weren't eligible to audition for the School Play "because of those boring old exams," as Bella put it. Most of all, though, we talked about boys. Bella said that night, "I can't think why I bothered with that Simon Findlay. I don't think he's up to much. I mean, he looks all right, but a bit weedy, and he hasn't got much to say for himself. A scientist! How boring!"

Bella considered that only artists were interesting. It didn't much matter what the art was, but she did insist on pallor, squalor, beards, dirty fingernails, and general suffering. Jazz musicians were best, because of the deliciously late hours they kept.

"As it happens," she went on, dismissing the subject of Simon Findlay (and leaving me to try and work out how I could get the conversation back to him. I wanted to know exactly what he'd said and done every second he was with Bella), "I did meet these absolutely amazing men."

"Were they really men?" Alice wanted to know. "You always call them that and then they turn out to be about fourteen."

"No, no." Bella was so excited that she sat up in bed. "Honestly! Men is what they are. There's not one of them under twenty-five. Some must be nearly thirty."

"Why are there so many of them?" I said.

"Because they're a band, silly!" Bella laughed. "Don't you want to hear all about how I met them?"

"Go on," I said, "get on with it. Is it a good story?"

"Tremendous. Listen to this. D'you remember Nigel Warren? That cousin of Jennifer Black's ... you must remember ... Anyway, he'd taken me to this amazing dance. Some friend of his had a sister who was having a coming-out party. That bit's all boring so I'll skip to where a whole group of us went off after the dance to The Establishment."

"What's that?" asked Alice. "It sounds like a bank."

"Alice, I despair!" cried Bella. "How can anyone not know what The Establishment is? Don't you read *Private Eye*? Haven't I told you about *Beyond the Fringe*? The Establishment is a nightclub. They have a satirical cabaret. Everyone goes to The Establishment."

"Oh," said Alice quietly. *Private Eye* was beyond her. She'd told me so herself. She couldn't understand it properly, she'd said, and anyway the ink it was printed with came off on your hands. And it looked so messy.

"Anyway," Bella said, "there we were at The Establishment and Nigel was getting a bit . . . you know . . . demanding."

"Tell us," I said.

"Well, you know, pressing up close during dances and saying these flirtatious things into my beehive, and I just knew that he was going to dance me into a corner and kiss me, and, quite honestly, I hated the thought of that."

"I thought you quite liked Nigel Warren," I said.

"Enough to go to a dance with, but not enough to kiss. So, I excused myself and said I had to go to the Ladies, and then I left him. He went back to where all the others were sitting and I went to find a lavatory." Bella paused. She often paused at moments of special drama. We knew our cues, though. We'd been having this kind of conversation for seven years.

"Then what happened?" said Alice.

"Then," said Bella, "I bumped into Pete. Literally. I opened the door of the Ladies and walked straight into him. It was almost as if it were meant. Destined." Bella sighed.

"What does he look like?" I asked.

"Tremendously dark. Bearded. Kind of sunken eyes. He was wearing jeans and a checked shirt and he had a cigarette burning . . . oh, he was so *thin!*" There was yearning in Bella's voice.

"He sounds awful," Alice said. "He could have been drunk or anything. He sounds . . . dangerous."

Bella laughed. "That's what I like about him. Anyway, it turned out that he was just leaving for what he called a 'jam session' with his band, and would I like to come and hear them? And so I did. I went off with Pete and met the other six members of the band in this little club called The Black Cat."

"What about Nigel? Didn't he mind?" You couldn't leave anything out when Alice was listening. She did like all loose ends to be neatly tied up.

"I just said good-bye and thank you and that I'd met this really old friend, etc., etc."

"Gosh!" Alice was impressed. "Weren't you scared? I'd have been terrified."

"You haven't met Pete. He is so clearly gentle and unterrifying."

"But the black hair and the beard and the sunken eyes!" I said. "You do make him sound like a pirate."

"Well, he isn't," Bella said. "He's kind and plays the saxophone. Anyway, don't you want to hear what happened next?"

"Go on," I said. I was getting a little bored. Bella's story didn't seem to be very exciting and it was getting late. I wasn't going to be able to steer the talk back to Simon. My eyelids drooped from time to time, but I heard the gist of Bella's story, the main parts . . . the band, and how nice they'd all been, and how she had sung with them.

"Imagine!" she said. "Me singing! 'Sweet Georgia Brown' and 'Danny Boy' and 'Blue Moon' with a *real* band! I've never had such fun in all my life, and the very best thing about it is they want me to sing with them again. They're playing for a dance at Coleston next month . . . for St. Valentine's Day. On a Saturday night. Will Herbie give me permission, d'you suppose?"

"To go and sing with a gang of bearded jazz musicians? You must be joking!" I said.

"That's what I thought," Bella said. "Well, I shall have to sneak out and sneak back . . ."

"You can't!" Alice shrieked. "You'll be expelled."

"They won't catch me. I'll get Pete to wait in the van at that road just through the forest. When I come back I can get through a downstairs window. The J.P.R. or something. You'll have to make sure to leave one open for me. We'll arrange it all most awfully carefully, don't worry. But isn't it exciting? Me, singing with a band?"

"What about Pete?" Alice asked. "Are you in love with him?"

"No," Bella said. "At least, I don't think so. But I shouldn't mind him kissing me. He hasn't got a soft, round, pink, rosebuddy kind of mouth like Nigel has. He's got a straight, firm sort of mouth."

"But the beard." Alice shuddered. "Ugh! Wouldn't the hair sort of get in the way?"

"I'll tell you," said Bella, "when I've done it. In Spain they say: A kiss without a mustache is like an egg without salt. It's true. Miss Clarke told us last year."

A silence fell while I wondered what I could say to turn the conversation back to Simon Findlay. Then Alice said into the darkness: "I've met a boy, too," and Bella and I both almost jumped out of bed.

"Oh, Alice," Bella said. "How could you let me go on and on! That's marvelous! Who is he? Where did you meet him? Have you kissed him? Tell us what he looks like. Tell us everything."

"There's not that much to tell," Alice said. "I've only just met him. The day before yesterday. He was staying with my aunt Lily. He comes from France, but he speaks such good English. He had an English nanny or something. He's called Jean-Luc. He's very fair. He's got blue eyes. I can't describe people like Bella, so that you can see them. All I know is, he's jolly handsome."

"How many times did you see him?"

"Once."

"And did he kiss you?"

"No, of course not. Don't be silly. How could he possibly have kissed me with Aunt Lily and his mother sitting in the drawing room with us?"

"Would you have liked him to kiss you?" Bella persisted.

"Oh, yes. Yes," Alice said, and although I couldn't see her, I felt sure she was blushing. "I keep thinking of what it will be like. I think about it over and over. What it will be like when he kisses me."

"So when is this kissing going to take place?" Bella asked. "When are you going to see him again?"

"I don't really know. He's gone back to France. But he'll write to me. He said he would. And I will write to him. We did swap addresses."

"Oh, hurray!" said Bella. "Honestly, Alice, you are slow! Couldn't you have kissed him good-bye or something?"

"No, but I could see from the way he looked at me that he wanted to. I might get a letter from him tomorrow. I shall ask him to my dance in the summer . . ." Alice's voice was

fading. She would be asleep in seconds. Bella
hadn't said anything for a few moments,
which almost certainly meant that she was
asleep, too. I was left alone to wonder when I
would see Simon Findlay again. Would he
come to Chapel in the morning? Perhaps I
could go and see Dorothy in the labs at break.
Perhaps.

LONDON *April 13, 1962*

Every day you get up early and go to your
work in the laboratory. I can't really imagine it
very clearly, and you never describe it. When I
think of it, I think of the labs at Egerton Hall.
If I'm all alone here, which I am for the most
part, I just stay in bed. It's perfectly comfortable for writing and also for reading, and it
does save money. The meter that provides gas
for the fire seems to gobble up the shillings.
Or sometimes, after I've finished my shift at
the coffee shop, we go to the pictures. It's so
lovely and warm there in the dark. Occasion-
ally, we share an ice-cream bar. *The Hustler* is
on, with Paul Newman in it. I'd love to see
that. Maybe we can go tonight.

Alice and Bella have both written to me.
They're coming to visit me next week, but not

together. Bella thinks what I've done is romantic—flight, escape, the search for freedom. Her letter is full of stuff like that. Also, love. As if love were the most important thing of all, more important than anything in the world. I used to think that, but now I'm not so sure. Perhaps love needs a whole arrangement of other things to support it, to keep it standing: a kind of scaffolding without which it simply falls to the ground in little shards and splinters. The scaffolding around Austen House, the pattern of metal bars and wooden planks between the ground and my window . . . how differently everything would have turned out if it hadn't been there!

English, French, and Spanish: those were (and maybe still are) my subjects. Bella's are the same as mine, and Alice's are nearly the same, only she's doing Art instead of Spanish.

There were only six of us in Miss Clarke's Advanced Spanish Class. We thought of ourselves as different, special, a cut above the others who were studying mundane subjects like Geography and Biology. Spanish most definitely had a touch of the exotic about it. Bella used to say she only did it because she could imagine herself so well in a red skirt covered with lace-edged flounces, and with a black mantilla cascading down over her hair. Part of this was Miss Clarke's doing. She assumed a good knowledge of the language because she had striven for four years, and made us learn lists of words, and recite verbs, and do exercises in translation from one language to another until we were more or less proficient. Now that we were in the Sixth Form, she, of all the staff, treated us as entirely grown-up and discussed everything with us as though we were equals. She was a stout, gray-haired lady who dressed in clothes more appropriate to a slender young girl: beads and floaty chiffon scarves and shoes in ridiculously light colors. Still, Bella and I (and Prue, Joanne, Nicola, and Alison) were agreed that Miss Clarke was a Woman of the World and well versed in sexual matters. She was, Bella asserted, "certainly not a virgin," or how could she possibly discuss Saint John of the Cross in the way she did?

"Most of these poems," Miss Clarke told us, "were written by Saint John during his imprisonment in Toledo in 1567. In a tiny prison cell. Imagine that, girls! A cell so small he could hardly turn around in it. And of course, in a poem such as the one beginning '*En una noche oscura*' . . . translate, please, Megan."

"Once, on a dark night," I said.

"Good, good," Miss Clarke continued. "It is clear, is it not, that although Saint John is speaking of the mystical union of the Soul with God, the *language* he uses is that of human physical love. This is the only way he can convey the sheer ecstasy that losing himself in God brings, do you see? Of course, you do have to remember that he is writing from a man's point of view. Now," she swept a stray end of wispy scarf over her shoulder, "Alison, find me two examples of physical images in the poem."

"Um," Alison murmured. She was a careful girl, and Bella said she wasn't altogether sure that Alison knew the meaning of the word 'ecstasy.' "I think . . . '*El rostro recliné sobre el Amado . . .*'"

"Good," Miss Clarke said. "'I laid my face upon my Lover.' That's clear enough. Another, please."

"'*Con su mano serena . . . ,*'" Alison began, and Miss Clarke interrupted her.

"Yes, yes, yes, *of course*. Listen to the whispering *s*'s, the gentle stroking of them! Read the lines aloud, please, child, so that we can all thrill to them."

Alison sounded dreadfully embarrassed.

> *"Con su mano serena*
> *En mi cuello hería*
> *Y todos mis sentidos suspendía,"*

she stammered.

"No, no, no, child!" Miss Clarke cried. "You make it sound like a laundry list. Can't you *hear* the music? It's even there in the English. I shall read it in Roy Campbell's translation. He, of course, is a poet in his own right. Now listen."

Miss Clarke stood up and her hand fluttered in the air. She seemed almost to be swooning as she said the words in English:

> "With his serenest hand
> my neck he wounded and
> suspended every sense with its caresses."

Later, we all agreed that what with burning hearts and love flowering in his breast, and the Lover and the Bride transfigured each into the other, Saint John of the Cross was certainly putting forward a very convincing picture.

"I don't know," Joanna said after the lesson. "There's an awful lot of it about in poetry and things. I mean, are we supposed to mention it in essays in the exams? I'm not sure I actually know what he's going on about all the time. Maybe because of what Miss Clarke said about him being a man. Perhaps it's different for women."

"It isn't all that different," Bella said. "I know exactly what he means. I've had lots of caresses that have suspended every sense!"

"But what's all that about wounding your neck with his hand?" said Prue. "That doesn't sound too pleasant." She giggled.

"It's just like that, though." Bella was always glad to enlighten us lesser mortals, the ones with no experience to draw on. "It honestly is. Sometimes when they touch you . . . you know . . . in certain places . . . well, it feels as though you're being burned, set on fire."

"How frightful!" Prue didn't like the sound of that at all. Bella sighed. "There's no hope for you, Prue Simpson," she said. "Go down to the lacrosse field and chuck the ball about."

"Lots more fun than fainting away among the lilies."

Prue smiled in a good-natured way and went off to her healthy activities. The rest of us stayed in the classroom for a bit, discussing whether or not Saint John of the Cross could possibly have known what he was writing about from personal experience. Bella thought he must have done, but I thought he could have made it all up. After all, I'd written pretend love poems by the dozen, and I had never been near a boy in my life. Now that I really loved someone, though, the usual love words wouldn't appear in what I was writing. I think I was shy of making the marks on the paper. That would be like putting up a sign for all to see. That afternoon, I was alone in the study I shared with Alice and a no-nonsense pony-lover called Marion Tipton, who just happened to be a brilliant mathematician as well. Our study was always full of people. Bella, for instance, was almost always in there, bringing her radio with her.

"Radio Luxemburg is too noisy for some people," she would sigh. "Some people think themselves too high and mighty for rock 'n' roll."

This was a reference to Mary-Ellen Walker, who was, in our opinion, snobbish and silly and had won our undying contempt in Junior House, when she would never answer to "Mary."

"My name is Mary-Ellen," she would simper to girls and staff alike. Bella always called

her "Our Ellie" to her face, and Mary-Ellen
had grown used to this over the years, but she
and Bella had never grown to like one another, and it was a stroke of bad luck that had
them sharing a study. What it meant was that
Bella did most of her prep sitting in an armchair wedged between my desk and Alice's,
and quite often there'd be Jerry Lee Lewis in
the background telling us (as if we didn't
already know) that there was a whole lot of
shakin' goin' on. But that day, Bella was taking
prep in the J.P.R. and Alice was in the Art Studio, "getting the draperies right" as she put it,
on her clothed figure drawing. I was studying
my French: reading through *Phèdre* and making notes on her character. The light of what
had been a bright, frosty day was disappearing,
and the sky was exactly as I liked it best: turning all sorts of beautiful colors—blue, and
pearly mauve, and finally an opalescent gray
just before the dark fell, against which the out-
lines of Eliot House stood out like black paper
cutouts. In the Eliot House studies, lights had
been switched on. Some people were quick to
draw their curtains, but some had left them
open and I could look in and see what they
were doing. Marcia Willis was putting up a
bullfighting poster. Someone I couldn't see

had their feet, still wearing lacrosse boots, up on the windowsill. Out of the corner of my eye I saw two figures coming down the steps of Main School and turned to see who they were. It was Fiona Mackenzie and Simon Findlay, and they were walking directly toward my window. Where were they going? What were they talking about? I drew the curtains across the window and sat down, trembling. Then I stood up and turned the light out, pushed my fingers between the curtains to make a tiny gap, and looked out. Fiona had her face turned toward Simon Findlay all the time, and he was looking at her. They disappeared around the corner of the building. Was Fiona going to take him to her study in Browning House and give him shortbread from a tin? I sat down at my desk in the dark and felt like crying. If Fiona was interested in the new lab assistant, then he certainly wouldn't notice me, wouldn't even know I existed. Fiona was tall and slender with an abundance of dark curls spilling over the collar of her school blouse. She was Deputy Head of Browning, Captain of Netball and Lacrosse, and had the whitest, straightest teeth you ever saw outside a Macleans advertisement.

Moreover, she was doing three sciences for

A-level and scarcely had a lesson outside the labs. I was no competition for Fiona. It wasn't until I'd said that to myself that I realized how much I wanted to be the one that was loved, the special one, the one to catch the attention of this, the most beautiful young man I'd ever seen.

"You're a fool," I said aloud and then again just to make sure I'd heard myself the first time, "A bloody stupid, idiotic fool!" I simply wanted to be in love, that was all, and it probably wouldn't have mattered a bit what he was like. I'd made up my mind to fall in love the moment Dorothy had told me about him. I could see that now. It was almost as though I had become a cave: dark and empty and all ready to have the first wave rush up the beach and flood me, fill me up with love like foamy seawater. That was what he was, this Simon Findlay: the first wave. The first man I had ever seen, the first person who wasn't a schoolboy or someone's spotty brother, and he had looked up at my window, and that was that. I thought of telling Bella how I felt, but I knew what she'd say. "You don't get out enough. You don't meet enough people. You're practically as bad as Alice."

I switched the light on again and turned

back to my work. Forget him, I said to myself.
Fiona has got him and you've got exams. Concentrate, I said to myself. Think of poor
Phèdre, also suffering the torments of love . . .
but I couldn't. I took out the poem I'd written
the night before and tinkered with it a little
and added a bit to it. It made me feel better,
doing that. By the time the bell went for supper, the poem looked like this:

> I was in the window
> and you turned, looked up
> to see the frame around my face.
>
> You were too far down
> and leaving. Walking
> toward the fountain
> where silver fish rise
> from the green circle
> of the nymphs' arms.
>
> I waited,
> a portrait of myself
> in the frame of the window.
>
> Now,
> the solid brick of roof and wall,
> gable and chimney, have thinned
> to paper cutouts, stuck
> on a pearl-gray sky.

You passed my darkened window
and didn't know
that it was mine,
that I was watching you
and that I stood against the wall
trying to disappear.

By the time I turned the light on,
the dark had covered you.

The next afternoon, Alice and I were walking along the paths between the lacrosse fields and the netball courts. Bella was playing netball, which for some reason I couldn't really understand she enjoyed, but Alice and I were going for a short walk instead. Games were mostly optional now that we were in the Sixth Form, and as far as I was concerned, that was almost the best thing about not being in the lower forms anymore. I shuddered when I remembered how I had hated it: the cold, the pointless running through mud, my total inability to manage that ridiculous contraption of wood and leather called a lacrosse stick, and the scorn of everyone trying to play the game around me.

"Buck up, Megan! Pass, for goodness' sake, Megan!" the other girls used to shout, and

Miss Robbins used to steam up behind me, her leathery cheeks flushed, her silver whistle bobbing about on the front of her Aertex shirt, and shriek, "Run, Megan! Faster! Pick your feet up!"

Tears of rage would spring into my eyes at this. Did she think I *could* run faster than I was running already? Couldn't she see that I was practically exploding? I hate her, I hate her, I used to think. I wish it would rain. I wish I could twist an ankle, break a leg, anything.

It was only about two years ago that I suddenly realized that Games didn't matter. I could be good at something else. There was no disgrace in not being very athletic and a snail-like runner. We were allowed to sign the Health Book, as it was called, when we were having a period, and be excused from Games. In the Fifth Form, the gap between my periods became shorter and shorter until it had disappeared altogether. Miss Herbert had summoned me to her study.

"You have, Megan dear," she said, "a somewhat unusual pattern of menstruation." She smiled. I couldn't think of a word to say.

"I take it," she continued, "that you are, in fact, quite well?"

I nodded.

"Then this is clearly a ploy to be excused from Games."

I nodded again.

"Very well. I shall have a word with Miss Robbins and her staff. You will go for walks during Games lessons in future. Is that more agreeable to you?"

"Oh, yes, Miss Herbert. Thank you very much."

Miss Herbert smiled again. "Fresh air, my dear, and some small movements of the limbs . . . far more ladylike than all that rough and tumble in the mud."

"Oh, far more ladylike," I agreed and bounded out of the study to tell the others.

I thought about this interview as Alice and I listened to the shouts of the players rising into the frosty air. They were running up and down on the churned-up grass, their thighs pink from the cold, the white ribbons of their breath curling up out of their mouths and fly- ing in the air. Alice wrapped her cloak tightly around her and shivered.

"Only another three days and then it's exams," she said. "I really don't know if I've done enough work. I'm so worried."

"You don't have to worry, Alice, honestly," I said. "You're one of the hardest workers I know. You always have been. You do everything so carefully, so methodically. You always have, ever since Junior House. Everyone knows that."

"Yes, but . . ." Alice looked at the ground. "I find it all . . . I don't know . . . hard. I don't know how to make a good answer out of what I know. I mean, I know I know it all, because I've learned it, but when the time comes to put it down, I can't somehow seem to get it all into the right size. I feel as if I'm cramming a huge lump of squashy dough into a little bin. I push a bit down here and another bit swells out there. I have nightmares about it, honestly."

"Oh, Alice, don't worry!" What could I say? I knew Alice was terrified of exams, but I didn't know what the right words were, the ones that would cheer her up. "It's only because we're friends with Bella that we notice it so much, but Bella's . . . well, she's different. Most people are more like you. Frightened. Or nervous at least. I know I am."

"Are you really?" Alice looked a little more cheerful. "I don't know how Bella does it, do you?"

"No," I said, "she's amazing."

It was true. For seven years, I'd come close to hating Bella at exam time. She'd be putting her hand up for more paper before you'd covered two sides, and she regularly finished ten minutes before the time was up and generally sat there staring round the room, smiling if you happened to look up at her. When she was younger, she used to use the point of her compass to clean under her nails, but that habit had mercifully been dropped. The really galling part about it all was how well Bella always did with what was the minimum of effort. I did well, too, I know, but I had to work for it. I suppose I should have been thankful that Dorothy had brought me up to study carefully and to organize my time, and that my own teachers had made me love what it was that I was working on for the most part, but still, I agreed with Alice, it was difficult not to feel resentful of Bella when exams came around.

"Anyway," I said to Alice in an attempt to cheer her up still further, "exams aren't everything. You have talents. Gifts for all sorts of things . . . and beauty."

"Do you think so, really?" Alice looked so grateful. It always astonished me that someone as artistic and lovely as she was should be so unsure about almost everything.

"Yes," I said, noticing how her golden red

hair was blowing in strands across the perfectly pink and white skin of her face, how her
gray eyes weren't really gray at all but like the
sea on a stormy day: gray and green and blue
all at once. "Yes, you have all the gifts, Alice,
and it is quite clear to me that exams or no
exams, you will live happily ever after."

"I feel a lot better now, Megan. You *are*
nice!"

"I feel as if I've been blown inside out," I
said. "Let's go in."

I'd managed to steer us to the back of the
Science Block. In order to reach School Corridor for the next lesson, we would have to
pass behind the labs. The labs had enormous
windows and Simon might be there, pouring
sinister-looking liquids into round-bottomed
flasks or something. Maybe we would see him.
I would have to look without Alice noticing
that I was looking. I would tell them about it, I
thought, if there were anything to tell, but just
this great, damp bundle of unrequited and
unrequitable love—why should anyone, even
my best friends, want to know about that?

"I think," said Alice, "I'll just go into the
Studio for a minute. You go on ahead, and I'll
see you in English."

This was a stroke of luck. I wouldn't have been able to look at Simon Findlay as carefully, as lovingly as I wanted to, if Alice had been there. I took my time walking along. Two labs seemed to be empty. Dorothy was teaching Fourth Formers in a third, and Simon Findlay was nowhere to be seen. I felt ridiculously disappointed, realizing that it had been my intention all afternoon to walk along this path at this time solely in order to catch a glimpse of him. I was in a worse condition than ever. I watched myself sliding deeper and deeper into a pool of feelings that were threatening to overwhelm everything else. The proof was that I had hardly given my work or the exams any thought at all. But where was he? With Fiona, I said to myself, and felt jealousy rising in my throat like bile. There was a ten-minute break before English. If I went into the labs and walked around, I could at least be in the place where he worked, touch the things that he touched, look at his lab coat, perhaps, hanging on a peg on the back of the door.

I've never thought of laboratories as particularly romantic places. When I was younger and doing Chemistry, I regarded them as chilly and smelly and unwelcoming, but oh, the transforming power of love! This lab, where Simon Findlay's coat was indeed hanging on the back of the door, seemed to me to be a kind of fairyland, an enchanted place where the glass bottles, jars of crystals and powders and liquids the color of jewels, dishes and pipettes and retorts and clamps and Bunsen burners all glowed with a radiance I'd been too stupid to notice before. I walked over to the sink where a rack of test tubes was standing on the draining board. They had only just been washed. Drops of water still hung like small pearls along their sides. Maybe Simon Findlay himself had washed them.

"Hello," said a voice suddenly, and I turned and in spite of looking for him, planning to see him, wanting to speak to him, going over and over in my mind the exact words I would use when I *did* see him, I was still so surprised that I nearly knocked the test tubes into the sink.

"Oh, gosh, I'm so sorry," I said, catching them.

"That's quite all right. No harm done, is there?" Simon Findlay walked right over to where I was standing. He was no more than a foot away from me. I suppose it must have been my imagination, but I thought for a moment that I could feel a warmth coming from his body. Certainly I could smell him. He smelled different from anyone else I'd ever been near. Part of it was cigarette smoke in his clothes—a smell I recognized from being near Bella and Marjorie. Part of it was probably a laboratory smell of one kind or another, but not unpleasant: rather sharp and astringent. Maybe it was also his clothes, the tweedy smell of his jacket, but most of it I knew was him— his skin, the blood going round in his veins, his flesh. I almost fainted.

"Haven't I seen you before?" he said, looking at me rather carefully. I didn't dare look into his eyes, and I pretended suddenly to find a deeply intriguing speck on the linoleum.

"Look at me," he said. "I'm sure you're familiar."

I fixed my eyes on his face. I could see every pore of his skin. I could have counted his eyelashes.

"Got it!" he said. "The damsel in the Tower. The one with the golden hair falling over the windowsill. I knew I'd seen you. Hang on, I even remember your name. Mary. No, May . . . no, I'll get it in a sec. It's just on the tip of my tongue . . ."

I put him out of his misery. "Megan. Megan

Thomas," I said, and because I didn't know exactly what to say or do next, I started babbling on about Dorothy and how she was my guardian and how I lived here during the holidays as well. On and on I went and even as I spoke I wondered how I was ever going to stop.

But he stopped me.

"So you're what Dolly Dragon . . . gosh, I'm frightfully sorry . . . that's my name for her . . ."

I giggled. "That's all right. It's a jolly good name, actually. It suits her."

"She calls you 'her charge.' She did tell me all about you. She seems to be very fond of you."

I was immediately ashamed. "I know. I shouldn't really giggle when you call her a dragon. It's disloyal. She's been very kind to me. She's looked after me for years and years and I'm being ungrateful. It's just . . ."

"That she's not exactly . . . ," he said, and paused.

"What you'd call lovable or cuddly," I finished his sentence.

This started a new paroxysm of laughter. In the middle of it, I noticed that a queue of Second Formers had lined up outside the door.

"Look," I said, "I have to go now or I'll be

late for English, and there's a class waiting to come in here."

"This is an absolutely impossible place in which to have any kind of civilized conversation, isn't it? No sooner do things become interesting than a bell goes, alas, alack . . . but I do hope we'll have a chance to chat again sometime?"

"Oh, yes," I said. "I hope so, too."

I left the laboratories and floated down the stairs that led to School Corridor. Then I walked along it as quickly as I could to English, Simon's words (he had magically been transformed to "Simon" in my head) lingering sweetly in my ears. "No sooner do things become interesting." That means he thinks I'm interesting, or was he only being polite? He didn't have to say that, or the bit about wanting another chat, and he remembered who I was. He forgot your name, said another, more sensible voice in my head. But he knew *me*, I answered this sensible voice firmly. He recognized my face, which he only saw for a minute, and right up there in the window of the Tower Room . . . far away, and he recognized me.

Miss Doolittle had started the lesson and was not best pleased at my lateness.

"Really, Megan, if this is the attitude to

your classes you're displaying a few days before the examination, then it's most regrettable."

"I'm sorry, Miss Doolittle. I had to go back and fetch my Keats. I'd left it behind, you see."

"Very well, Megan. Sit down now and let us continue. We are discussing Keats's appeal to the senses: sight, sound, touch, and so on, in 'The Eve of St. Agnes.' Please go on reading, Susan." Susan Martin, a silent, rather plump girl, started to read:

> "And still she slept an azure-lidded sleep,
>   In blanchèd linen, smooth, and lavender'd,
>   While he from forth the closet brought a
>   heap
>   Of candied apple, quince, and plum, and
>   gourd;
>   With jellies soother than the creamy curd,
>   And lucent syrops, tinct with cinnamon;
>   Manna and dates, in argosy transferr'd
>   From Fez; and spicèd dainties every one,
>   From silken Samarcand to cedar'd
>   Lebanon."

I looked at Susan as she read and wondered if she was imagining herself to be Madeline and someone she knew to be Porphyro. Bella pushed a note into my hand. It said: "D'you think Dooly realizes what's going on in stanza 36? Is it right to feed such sexy stuff to impressionable girls? Great balls of fire! Pant, pant!" I looked at the lines in question:

> Ethereal, flush'd and like a throbbing star . . .
> Into her dream he melted, as the rose
> Blendeth its odour with the violet,—
> Solution sweet . . .

I winked at Bella. She was right, though. Between Keats and Saint John of the Cross, it did rather look as though the examiners were conspiring to make our young hearts beat faster. I spent the next few minutes in a dream of myself as Madeline, running along the tapestried halls with my lover.

> "The arras, rich with horseman, hawk, and
>   hound,
> Flutter'd in the besieging wind's uproar;
> And the long carpet rose along the gusty floor."

Susan finished reading the poem. Miss Doolittle pushed her gold-rimmed glasses more firmly on to the bridge of her nose and stood up.

"Well, girls, are we agreed that John Keats is a poet who appeals to the senses?"

Nods and yesses came from every corner of the room.

"Very well, then. Now it is up to us to discover exactly how it is he achieves these effects . . ."

I tried to do two things at once: to listen and learn so that perhaps I could borrow some of Keats's recipe for luscious poetry and put it into lines of my own, and also to shut my ears so that knowing how he put it together would not spoil the magic, break the spell that those words in just that order were capable of casting over me. I wondered briefly if Simon ever read poetry. I blushed when an image of him reading my poems came into my mind. A peal of laughter broke into my dreams.

"No, Bella," Miss Doolittle was saying, "'azure-lidded sleep' does *not* mean that Madeline has failed to remove her eyeshadow. I would urge you to be serious, girl. What *does* it mean? Yes, Angela?"

"It means her skin is very white and you can see the blue veins on her eyelids."

"Precisely. Thank you. And why do you think he uses these place-names: Fez, Samarkand, Lebanon? What sort of image do they conjure up in your mind?"

The lesson continued. At the end of it, I

walked along School Corridor with Bella. She
said, "I think we ought to have a sort of practi-
cal English lesson. Male volunteers to show us
what it means, all that stuff about blending the
rose and the violet. We'd be able to write
much better about Keats, if we knew about all
that."

The following day, Bella and I walked back to
school from the Games fields with Fiona
Mackenzie. Simon drove past us in his car and
waved cheerily.

"There's that rather divine young lab assistant," said Fiona.

"D'you think he's divine?" asked Bella. "I
thought he was a bit feeble, actually. Not my
type."

"Oh, no, he's not feeble at all," Fiona was
quick in her defense. "He's most awfully nice.
Friendly. I see quite a lot of him in the labs,
one way and another. He walked all the way
down to my study with me the other day, and I
was going to give him a cup of tea and a biscuit
when Miss Bates came bustling down the corridor behind us and scared him off . . . but I
really like him, and"—she winked at me and
Bella—"I think he quite likes me."

I had kept quiet during this conversation,

but this was too much for me. I said, "Did he say anything? To make you think he likes you, I mean? Or do anything?"

I could feel, as I waited for Fiona's answer, my heart fluttering about like a bird beating its wings against my ribs.

"No, nothing in particular," said Fiona, turning into the Browning House Study Passage. "Still, it's only the first week of term, isn't it? Lots of time . . ."

After she had gone, I went over my earlier conversation with Simon. What I had thought of as something glorious and shining and hopeful had been reduced to a tarnished little scrap of nothing very much.

LONDON *April 15, 1962*

I wonder how grown-up you have to be to stop thinking of a year as being divided up into terms and holidays? The word "week" when I say it to myself, brings to mind a printed timetable such as we filled in at the beginning of every term, with the times of the lessons printed down the left-hand side, the names of the days at the top of seven columns going from left to right, and two thick black lines separating the morning from the afternoon.

We always started exams on a Monday morning (top left-hand corner) and by the time we'd reached the bottom right-hand corner, they were generally over. Those were school exams, though. Public exams, A-level exams, will be dotted about all over the sheet and will go on for weeks. There will be whole days between one paper and another, and the sun will shine as it always does during exams, and we (they?) will lie around on the grassy slopes leading down from the terrace and pretend to be studying. I remember it from other years, from watching other girls doing it, summer after summer. When Bella, Alice, and I first came up from Junior House, we couldn't really believe that we would ever be quite as grown-up as that. And now, here I am, exactly the same as those girls were when I admired them and wondered at them. I can't think why I feel so childish and ignorant and bewildered. There are days when I would be relieved to see Dorothy marching in here and saying: "Enough of this nonsense, child, you're coming back home with me." On other days, I fear that she might actually do it. But she won't. She'll say nothing and write nothing and just wait for me to . . . what? Come to my senses? Disappear without a trace? Sometimes

I wonder if she'll ever forgive me, and at other times I wonder whether I actually need to be forgiven, whether what I've done is so dreadful after all. Dreadful or not, Dorothy is hurt by what we did.

It seems to me miraculous that I managed to pass the exams, let alone do quite well. That week (which is actually only about eight weeks ago) seems to belong to another lifetime, and when I think of myself then, it's as though I'm looking at a stranger, someone I hardly know. What I mainly remember is a feeling of being two quite separate people, all the way through the week before the exams started.

"Schizophrenia," said Bella knowledgeably. This was the night before the first exam, and up in the Tower Room after lights-out. I had just told Alice and Bella about my longing for Simon, and how thinking about him seemed to have cut me in half. I used to crane my neck in Chapel to see where he was sitting and could he see Fiona and were looks passing between them. I used to go for long walks along the Rim of the Known World, peering into the spaces between the trees, expecting at any moment to see him come sauntering out, his arm around Fiona's waist. . . . It was a lover and his lass, with a hey and a ho and a hey nonny no. I would go and see Dorothy in the labs on almost any pretext in the hope of bumping into him. I don't know what Dorothy thought of this, because she always said so little. Still, she must have wondered, because over the years an understanding had grown between us: during the term, I was just another girl in the school. It was only during the holidays that Dorothy turned by magic into my adoptive mother. In my heart I regard her as only a guardian and never think of her as a real mother, and I don't know whether this is my fault or hers, but I do feel a certain guilt about it. She did try to be like a mother to me during the holidays, but it was as though she were copying maternal behavior she had seen in other people, and not quite succeeding. She was clumsy at domestic things, like going shopping together for clothes and shoes, and when we were alone, we talked or discussed or argued, but we almost never laughed. Small smiles were more Dorothy's sort of thing, and she seemed frightened of displays of emotion. There were times when I used to think that if she had had someone noisier, sillier, bouncier, and more loving than

me to look after, she would have been different, but it's futile to wonder such things after
all these years. We visited a great many muse-
ums during the holidays, and Dorothy was a
wonderful guide. She knew so much and
explained it so clearly and was so happy to see
me interesed that these visits remain in my
mind as the most pleasurable occasions of my
childhood. Dorothy was as contented as I was
in the long, quiet corridors. We could become
a teacher and a pupil again: roles in which we
were well rehearsed and confident.

Anyway, there I'd be, hanging around the
labs, and sometimes I'd be rewarded with a
glimpse of Simon. There were always droves
of giggling girls around his bench or helping
him to clean up the labs after a lesson, so I
never had a chance to speak. Once or twice,
though, he saw me and waved and smiled, and
on these occasions I went about in a dream of
bliss. Once, however, I thought I'd caught
sight of him going down the Browning House
Study Passage, and for the rest of that afternoon I was in agonies of grief and longing in
my study, imagining him and Fiona doing all
the sorts of things we'd read about in *Peyton
Place* and (oh, what anguish!) *Lady Chatterley's*

Lover. I explained all this to Alice and Bella at last, unable to bear it on my own.

"It's not only the love," I said. "It's everything else as well . . . working for the exams all the time and reading about all these other lovers . . . I can't concentrate properly. It's awful. I don't know how I'm going to keep my mind on what I'm writing for a whole three hours. I keep daydreaming."

"You must speak to him," Bella said. "Just march straight up to him and ask him to go for a walk with you, or something."

"She can't." Alice looked up, shocked. "Everyone'll see them. Dorothy would soon find out and then what would she say? She'd probably send Simon away."

"That's being feeble, Alice. I bet I could find a way. What about writing him a note? Invite him to Study Tea."

"What would I say in the note?" I asked.

Bella laughed, "Oh, I don't know . . . something informal and cool, like you're burning with love for him . . . your thighs are throbbing, your breast is heaving . . . that kind of thing."

I threw my pajama case at her. "Fat lot of use you are!" I groaned and punched my pillow into a more comfortable shape before lying down. "There's nothing to be done. I shall just have to languish. Languish and hope for the best."

"Maybe," said Alice, "the exams will take your mind off it a bit. I haven't even had time to answer Jean-Luc's letter."

Bella and I giggled. Jean-Luc's letters we privately thought of as disappointing. Alice obviously regarded them as real love letters, so we never disillusioned her, but to us they seemed very faint and lackluster in the Shining Words of Love department. As Bella put it, "You can hardly count *'mes amitiés'* or *'bien affectueusement,'* can you? I mean, there's not even a *'baisers'* to be found, much less a *'gros baisers.'* I don't think this Jean-Luc is up to much."

"Don't for heaven's sake tell Alice," I said. "She thinks they're marvelous. Haven't you seen how she peers at the pile of letters by Herbie's plate all through breakfast?"

It was true. Alice could hardly eat, so busy was she scrutinizing the pile. Miss Herbert always gave out the letters after she had eaten

a) cornflakes
b) a boiled egg

c) one triangle of brown toast, thinly spread
with butter and an almost invisible glaze
of marmalade.

If Alice's name was read aloud, she would
blush furiously and collect her missive with
trembling hands. I sometimes thought Alice
would eat more at breakfast if the letters were
read out first, but then there would be the tor-
ment of waiting until she was on her own to
open it.

Bella had been getting letters from the
band. The dance they were playing at was on
Saturday, February 17th.

"It's a Valentine's Day Dance," Bella told
us. "I've got it all arranged. They're going to
wait for me just the other side of the forest.
The van'll be parked on the main road to
Egerton Magna, and they'll bring me back the
same way."

"It'll be the Valentine's Day Massacre if
you're caught," I said.

"But I won't be. Listen, I've got it all
worked out. I'll say I've got a headache and
I'm going to have an early night. Then I'll
sneak out while you're all in the Hall for Saturday Night Dancing. No one ever comes up
here, Megan, you know that, and I'll be back

before morning. You leave the J.C.R. window open and I'll close it behind me. Don't look so worried, Alice. I'll leave pillows in my bed, just in case someone looks in. It'll be a jolly joke, just like the ones in those old school stories we used to read."

Alice and I didn't argue. It was no use arguing with Bella once she'd made her mind up. In order to sing with a real band at a real dance, she would have risked almost anything. Bella didn't even notice our silence. She went on, "And, I say, can you both come out with me this Sunday? I forgot to ask before. I had a postcard from Marjorie . . . they're coming to take me out and would I like to bring Megan and Alice? Do say you'll come. I can't bear going out with them all by myself . . . there's nothing to talk about. Go on, say you'll come."

Alice and I both said we would, and then we all stopped talking. Soon the others were asleep, but I stared at the ceiling, going over *Phèdre* in my head, imagining Simon in a toga.

Je sentis tout mon corps et transir et brûler,
Je reconnus Vénus et ses feux redoutables.

Me, too, I thought. I'm fainting and burning, too, and I may not be a seventeenth-century version of an ancient Greek queen, but I can recognize Venus's redoubtable fires when I'm feeling them, just the same as anyone else.

Next morning, the prospect of a week of exams made the whole Upper Sixth subdued. Even the knives and forks at breakfast were quieter. All the younger girls seemed to catch the nervousness and didn't dare address a Sixth Former at all. After breakfast, there was much last-minute consulting of notes, sharpening of pencils, and tucking of good luck mascots into pencil cases. Alice and Bella had received good luck cards from the Third Formers who admired them and would have to reward these kids with radiant smiles at lunchtime. Alice was pale and tense. I was tired. Only Bella seemed exactly the same as usual, humming Buddy Holly songs under her breath as she searched unhurriedly through her desk for a missing pen. I was in her study with her, helping her to look.

"Honestly, Bella! That's the kind of thing one ought to prepare in advance, one's pens and things. It's frightfully important," said Mary-Ellen. She, Mary-Ellen, had everything neatly organized and was only waiting for the bell.

"Not as frightfully important, Ellie, me old fruit," said Bella in the stage Cockney she always adopted simply to annoy Mary-Ellen, "as actually having something interesting to write with one's pen when one has found it! All the stationery in the world, Mary-Ellen, will not make up for your startling mediocrity."

"You're simply foul," said Mary-Ellen. "I don't know why I should have to sit here and be insulted."

"You don't," Bella answered calmly. "You can stand in the middle of Study Passage and I'll gladly insult you there . . . and here's my pen! What a stroke of luck!" She sailed past Mary-Ellen. "Don't be late for the first paper, now, will you?"

Mr. Page, the caretaker, and his assistants had been busy in the night, like the elves who helped the shoemaker. The Hall had been transformed. Scores of wooden desks had been brought up from the Nether Regions under the floor and arranged in long rows. The Proctor's desk was up on the stage, and on it there were alarming gray envelopes containing the question papers and high piles of foolscap paper with blue lines and red margins. Each sheet of paper had a hole in the top left-hand corner, through which we had to thread a small piece of string. Miss Peacock, a Geography teacher, was walking up and down in between the rows of desks even as we came in, putting out a little bit of string for each person. Miss Hardy, head of Math, was following her with paper, four sheets each. Bella would be putting her hand up for more before I'd finished the first question. I looked around the Hall at the windows set so high up that no one could possibly see out of them; at the velvet curtains that had once, probably, been bottle green, but had now faded to the color of pea soup; at the wooden boards painted with the golden names of past prefects, Head Girls, and other school worthies. I was a prefect. It was strange to think that after I'd left school, someone would sit here, at this very desk and read my name: Megan Thomas (1955–62). Portraits of Phoebe and Louisa Egerton, in puce and gray respectively, gazed down benignly on us from the back of the stage, and more visible than anything else in the room, a huge clock hung above the Founders' heads. Its face was as wide as a crater on the moon, and as each minute passed, the big hand moved with a click that was audible to everyone in all that silence.

Exam week passed. What a luxury to be able to dismiss it like that, in three words! All through that week I slept badly, worried by dreams of Simon and of turning over a question paper only to find algebra questions on it that I could never begin to answer. It was because I was tired that Miss Herbert excused me from Saturday Night Dancing and told me to go and rest quietly on my bed instead—"With a relaxing rather than an invigorating book, perhaps."

I was delighted. I hated Saturday Night Dancing, and so did Alice and Bella, although most of the younger girls enjoyed it, and we were all expected to go.

"It's so frightfully depressing," Bella used to moan. "All these middle-aged women, dressed up in their best—and it *is* their best: full-length brocade and tatty fur stoles and Lord love us, even a bit of lipstick—all of them sitting there on stiff chairs up on that stage doing what? Watching a whole lot of lumpy girls dancing around together, and not very well, either, 'cause they haven't quite worked out the steps and should the girl being the man be going forward or backward...oh, it's dreadful!"

"Then, sometimes," I'd add, "they actually

dance. As Herbie herself would say, '*horresco referens:* I shudder to relate.' Some brave soul, or someone who's been dared to, goes up there and asks one of the staff to dance. What do they talk about as they go round and round? The results of last week's test? Yesterday's netball match? World current affairs? It's embarrassing, that's what it is."

"It must be even worse for them than for us," Alice said. "I mean, they are grown-up . . . old, really. Don't you think they get reminded of dances they went to when they were young? They probably feel most awfully sad. I feel sorry for them, actually."

"Well, I don't," said Bella. "It's their own fault. They don't have to have it. They could invite some boys' school over here, or they could let us play Radio Lux and dance around on our own. I wouldn't mind that nearly so much."

But boys and Radio Lux were both regarded as disruptive, if not downright evil, so Saturday Night Dancing remained as it was. I was delighted, that night, to be alone in the Tower Room. It was a beautiful evening, with the full moon floating in a wide pool of its own light. I opened the window, even though it was cold, and looked at the silvery limbs of the nymphs and the fish. I could hear fainter music lying over the music I was listening to on my transistor. It was coming from the Hall, but it sounded distant and sweet and unconnected with undignified shuffling around on the parquet floor. Then I heard the scrunch of gravel, and I sprang away from the window and felt a tremor of something like fear. Surely no one should be walking around at this time? Perhaps it was one of the maids, going home after washing up hundreds and hundreds of dirty plates. Yes, that was the most likely explanation . . . but I'd better have a look just in case.

If I hadn't thought in this way, if I hadn't gone to see, that night, whose were the noisy footsteps on the gravel, then . . . what? Would everything have been different? Would all that has happened in the last few weeks have taken place at all, let alone in exactly the way it did? I often think about that now, but then, I didn't hesitate. I went back to the window and looked down. The noise had stopped. Simon Findlay was standing at the bottom of the scaffolding.

"Hello," he said. "I saw the light on in your tower. I wondered if it was really you, or if the light had been left on by mistake. I was just about to call your name ... I saw Dorothy doing it the other day."

"Yes," I said. (Oh, such brilliant, sparkling conversation from someone who has lived and breathed for just this chance of a private talk!) "It is me. I've got a bit of a headache."

"Gosh, I am sorry."

"No, it's practically gone now, honestly."

"Good-oh! I say ..." Simon hesitated.

"Yes?"

"This is a bit stupid, isn't it? Me down here and you up there. We can't really talk. Not properly."

(Did he want to talk "properly"? What did that mean? My heart had jumped into my throat, so that I had some difficulty in answering him at all.)

"It can't be helped, I suppose," I stammered.

"'Course it can be helped. I'll come up," he said, and before I could say anything to stop him, he had begun to climb up the scaffolding. I watched him coming nearer and nearer. Soon I could see the individual hairs on the top of his head, and then his face was level with mine.

"Aren't you going to ask me in?" He was

grinning. "After I've come all this way to see you?"

"Come in," I said, and he climbed over, into the Tower Room, and stood next to me. I could feel myself trembling all over.

"I say," he said, "you're not scared of being caught, are you?"

I was, but I wasn't going to admit it. In any case, it wasn't the fear that was causing the trembling so much as his nearness, and the fact that the three beds were the only places in the room where we could sit. I shook my head.

"Don't worry," he said. "First sign of trouble and I'm down that scaffolding like a cat burglar."

"They won't be coming back for at least an hour," I whispered. "It's Saturday Night Dancing."

"What's that?" Simon said. "May I sit on this bed?"

"Yes, do."

He sat down on Alice's bed, and I sat down on my bed facing him. The tips of his brown suede shoes were only inches away from mine on the mauve rug. Our knees were almost touching. I began to tell him about Saturday Night Dancing and why Bella and Alice and I found it so depressing. On the transistor, Bobby Darin began to sing "Lazy River."

"May I have the pleasure?" Simon said and stood up. "This is one of my favorite songs, and I don't see why you shouldn't have a dance, even though you've got a headache."

"What? Here?" I'd have given anything to have been able to take back the words. How silly they were! How completely and devastatingly unromantic!

"Absolutely," Simon said, and he took hold of me in just the way we had been taught the gentleman takes hold of the lady. How strange we must have looked, dancing in between the beds and around the chest of drawers! I can see that now, but at the time I thought I was going to die of pleasure. He was holding me very close to him. Every bit of my body from my head down to my knees could feel a part of his body touching it. The thought flew into my mind: How am I going to tell Bella and Alice exactly what this feels like? I didn't have to talk. Simon was humming along with Bobby Darin. I could feel his lips moving softly in my hair. What does this mean, I kept thinking. Does it mean anything? Everyone has to touch when they dance, don't they?

This is what the gentlemen do . . . this is what the ladies do . . . it doesn't need to mean anything at all. Then the music stopped and Simon didn't let me go. I was dizzy. I was going to faint. I felt a blush spreading up all over me, all over my face. I stared down at the floor, but he put his hand under my chin and forced me to look at him. I knew what was going to happen next. He was going to kiss me.

"I'm going to kiss you," he said. "If you don't mind, that is." I couldn't speak. I just closed my eyes and waited. He kissed me very softly on the lips, so that I could hardly feel it, but I smelled his smell in my nostrils, and his hands were on my shoulders. I opened my eyes.

"I've been wanting to do that," he smiled, "ever since I first saw you at the window."

What could I say? Yes, and I've been longing, longing, longing for you to touch me?

"Was that the first time that you've been kissed?"

I thought about lying for one wild moment, but in the end I said, "Yes."

"And how old are you?"

"I shall be eighteen in April."

"Tsk, tsk. Whatever have you been doing for the last couple of years?"

"Nothing. I've just been here."

"Up in your tower," he smiled. "Come and sit down beside me on the bed. I want to kiss you again. Properly."

I think perhaps I had not been kissed enough in my life. My parents, even in my earliest childhood, were not much given to touching and hugging, and Dorothy had hardly ever kissed me at all: a peck on the cheek for good-bye and a similar one for hello each time I went to stay with Alice or Bella. Therefore, I was unprepared for what Simon meant by kissing. Listening to Bella and others whom I thought of as "more experienced" and reading all the right books with particular emphasis on the "good bits," I had always thought that kisses came rather low on the scale of possible excitement. But as Simon began to place small, fluttery kisses on my neck and eyelids, and deeper, longer kisses on my lips; as he persuaded my lips to part and touched my tongue with his, I began to feel as though every single one of my nerve ends was singing with pleasure. I was aware of nothing but Simon. It was as though I were drowning:

drowning and falling at the same time. I could hear my own heart hammering in my body— or was it his? All sense of where I was, or what time it was, or other people, disappeared. The whole universe was now entirely contained in my body, and every beautiful feeling in the world was blossoming and uncurling under my own burning skin, over my flesh, and in my mouth made moist and tender by his kisses.

"I think," I gasped when Simon stopped for a moment, "I must have died and gone to heaven."

"It gets better," he answered. "This is only the beginning . . . oh, I shall show you such things . . ."

That means, I thought to myself, that he wants to see me again. That this isn't just a momentary aberration.

"It's going to be awfully difficult," I murmured. "I don't think a girls' boarding school is the ideal place for . . . this sort of thing."

"How unadventurous you are!" Simon smiled. "It's absolutely perfect. There is an added element of mystery and danger. Keeping things secret rather adds to the fun, doesn't it?"

"Yes, but where can we meet? It's too cold

to go out for long walks, and you couldn't come to my study. I share it."

"What's wrong with this room?"

"Here? But however would you get here?"

"Silly! Up the scaffolding, just like tonight."

"I can't have a headache every Saturday night, though, can I? They'll catch on, become suspicious."

"We'll find times. Evening prep. You can creep up here when you're meant to be in your study, and I'll meet you. Daytime's no good because of the workmen . . ."

"And you don't want anyone catching sight of you on their way back from Games or anything."

"Don't worry. I'll find a way to reach you. I must reach you. Oh, Megan, we're wasting what little time we have. Come here. I'm going to unplait your hair." I turned my back to him and closed my eyes. I could feel his fingers threading through my tightly braided hair, loosening it, shaking it out, then stroking it as if I were a cat, down from the crown of my head to where it hung nearly touching my waist. I could have gone on sitting like that for hours, but he pulled me round so that I was facing him again. He took me in his arms, and we forgot ourselves and wallowed in our kissing to such an extent that he had to leave in a great hurry. I leaned out of the window and watched him climbing down. I wanted to call out: "Come back. I love you. Stay with me. I want you," and other soppy things, but all I said was, "Good night." He didn't even answer properly, just waved and smiled. My hair fell in a stream over the sill as I leaned forward. I gathered it hastily into an elastic band. I almost never wore it loose, and Alice and Bella would be here soon. I looked into the mirror to see if I looked different, to see if it showed, the fact that I had been altered, all the atoms of my body rearranged into new patterns. Apart from the fact that my eyes were very bright, almost as if I'd been crying, and my cheeks were flushed, I looked just the same. I lay on my bed and waited for the sound of footsteps on the stairs. The stairs . . . I closed my eyes and imagined myself tiptoeing up them, up and up while everyone else was bent over their work. The main staircase of Austen House would be the secret hidden stairway of the heart that Saint John of the Cross describes: *la secreta escala disfrazada*, the one the Soul goes up on its way to Union with God:

En una noche oscura
con ansias en amores inflamada . . .

Well, the night would be dark when I went up, and all *my* cares would be blazing into love, and just as Saint John describes, the only light in all that darkness and silence would be the one burning, shining, leaping in my heart.

LONDON *April 17, 1962*

I should go to the laundromat, otherwise we will have no clothes to wear tomorrow. It's amazing, the things that are organized for you when you are a child and that you have to attend to all by yourself as a grown-up. Bella, so eager, so much wanting to be grown-up, let me tell you: it's not easy. Bella even gets taken to the hairdresser's by her stepmother at the end of every holiday, so as to be neat for school. I went with them once, when I was staying with Bella, and now, when I look in the mirror and see my hair in the same style I've worn since I was six years old, I am reminded of it. It was on that day, too, that I understood how little Bella had exaggerated when describing her stepmother to us.

I shall write about it first and attend to the dirty knickers later. How real life does get in the way sometimes!

Going to Armand's was one of the treats, one of the best things about staying with Bella during the holidays. In front of every seat there was an enormous mirror in an ornate, gilded frame, and the hairdressers, all robed in pink, wafted between the chairs like a cloud of butterflies. Bella, of course, was always attended to by Monsieur Armand himself. Marjorie, Bella's stepmother, had ensconced herself in one of the velvety armchairs in the reception area, but I sat in the chair next to Bella's and listened to everything that was going on. Monsieur Armand's eyes had lit up when he saw my hair; he had such dreams of snipping and curling, you could almost see the scissors twitching, but Bella said, "It's no use, Armand, looking at that plait. Silly old Megan insists on the Rhine-maiden look and there's nothing to be done about it."

Armand sighed deeply, making me feel as though I were letting the side down.

As he combed out Bella's hair, she said,

"Come on, Armand, just a bit more bouf-
fant . . . just a weeny bit."

"But, mam'zelle, she say . . . your mother
say . . ."

Bella put her tongue out, and she and
Armand giggled together.

"She's not my mother, she's my stepmother. Go on, while she's not looking. A tiny
bit more backcombing should do it."

Armand shrugged and picked up his comb.
Bella, I thought to myself, will never be able to
put her school hat on top of that. She wouldn't
mind. She'd simply not wear it. Bella had
strong views on lots of things, and one of her
strongest views concerned the school uniform.

"It's cruelty," she used to explain to anyone
who would listen and frequently to those who
wouldn't. "It limits our freedom. Our individ-
uality. Our style."

"But it's a great leveler, dear," people
(teachers, mothers, etc.) used to say. Bella
would snort in reply. She was a great snorter.
Who wants to be level? she was thinking.

I glanced into the mirror. I could just see
Marjorie. She was hidden behind the *Tatler*
and only her hands were visible: long, dark
red fingernails and very white fingers scarcely

able to move about for the weight of rings, heavy gold-link bracelets, and other assorted baubles. Bella didn't like her much and enjoyed the fact enormously.

"Whatever's the point of a stepmother," she'd say, "if she isn't wicked?"

Marjorie wasn't exactly wicked. Not really. Even Bella admitted this. But she was small-minded, critical, and jealous of the relationship between Bella and her father, between this friend and that, and especially of the relationship that had once existed between Bella's father and mother. Well, she was a jealous person and that was that. She was also vain. Bella, it's true, was forever primping and preening and admiring herself, but, as she had once told us, me and Alice, "Marjorie's worse. Much worse. Once she tore up a dress that made her look fat. Honestly. Didn't even bother to let me try it on, to see if it suited me. I bet it would have done, too."

"*Voilà, mam'zelle.*" Armand stepped back, pleased with himself.

"*C'est formidable!*" Bella cried and turned to me. "Wouldn't Miss Donnelly be proud of me? Well, whatever's the point of French A-level, if I can't chat to Armand?"

Marjorie was summoned. She put down her

magazine and came over to the mirror. Then she leaned down so that her face was near Bella's in the glass.

"Very nice, dear," she said after staring for a long time. "But don't you think it's a little . . . too much for school, perhaps?"

I could hear the voice growing thin, sharpening a little.

"Oh, no," Bella said. "Not at all. Truly. It'll be fine."

"Very well, then." Marjorie patted her own sleek, golden brown pageboy hairstyle. "But honestly, Armand, tell us what you think. Which do *you* think looks prettier?" Marjorie was smiling now through glossy lips. Armand threw up his hands in a gesture of defeat.

"That is of the most difficult, such a choice. Of course, Madame is chic itself. This we all know, *naturellement*. And yet, I have to say, mam'zelle's style is . . . how do you say? The latest. *Le dernier cri.* Utmost modernity. *Enfin, Madame, c'est la jeunesse . . . qu'est-ce qu'on peut dire?*" He folded his arms in a gesture of resignation.

Marjorie hurried away to gather her furs from where they'd been hung up, and Bella said, "One in the eye for her, then. Silly old thing." She stood up to take her robe off. The mirror reflected no faces now, nothing but the movements of the butterfly-hairdressers and the row of silver dryers on the opposite wall. I thought about their faces, Bella's and Marjorie's, nearly touching in the mirror, and about the look in Marjorie's eyes when she compared her skin (golden with makeup but beginning to coarsen and wrinkle in spite of the best efforts of Elizabeth Arden) with Bella's, which seemed, in the rosy light of the salon, almost incandescent. And had Marjorie noticed the gray streaks just visible near her hairline? The almost blue sheen on Bella's hair, newly washed, set, and backcombed, must have struck her like a warning. She walked out of the salon so abruptly that we had to run to catch up with her. This happened two years ago, and I still remember it.

The day after Simon first climbed into the Tower Room, Alice and I were going out with Bella and her father and Marjorie. We found it hard to wake up when the bell went because we'd spoken so late into the night, analyzing every word and gesture of what Bella was calling, with capital letters in her voice, "Megan's Initiation." Alice always found it hard to wake up, and Bella and I were quite used to throwing wet washcloths at her, or stripping back the blankets, or tickling her feet.

"There's another aspect to all this," said Bella, pushing Alice's shoulder, "and that's the brilliant idea your Simon has given me. I shall climb up the scaffolding to this very room after the dance on the seventeenth."

"Bella, you can't! You'll fall and kill yourself."

"What rubbish! I could climb up that scaffolding as easy as winking. It's just never occurred to me before."

"But you're not seriously going to go and sing with this band, are you? I mean, you could be expelled if you're caught."

"Look who's talking. It's absolutely allowed, of course, to let young men have their wicked way with you in one of the school bedrooms."

"He hasn't had his wicked way with me . . . and anyway, I do wish you wouldn't put it like that."

"He will. Give him time. He's only been up here once. I bet you anything you like you'll be the first one of us to lose her virginity."

"I won't." I was blushing.

"Yes, you will," Bella said. I shook my head vigorously, but she went on, "Actually, I don't see anything so frightful about it. They can't expect us to read all these poems saying gather ye rosebuds and things like that, and then say, no, sorry, there won't be any rosebud-gathering after all, ducky, at least not until after you're married and quite respectable."

"But, what if you were to get pregnant?" I asked, suddenly terrified. What if Bella were right? Was I ready for this? Did I even want it?

"There are ways of preventing pregnancy, you know," Bella said.

"But no one tells us anything about them," I said. "It's not fair. They make us study all these love poems and then they don't tell us what to do about it."

"You should ask Simon. He's sure to know. He's a scientist."

"I'd die! I'd die of embarrassment. I mean, I don't really know him well enough."

Bella had stopped listening to me and was trying to lure Alice out of her sleep by murmuring things about Sunday breakfast into her ear. We had rolls and honey on Sunday mornings and bananas, too. We used to ask our banana a secret question, and then cut the end off it with a sharp knife. Sometimes, you could see a black Y shape very clearly and that meant the answer to your question was yes. Sometimes the fruit produced only a dot or an indeterminate blur, and that was a no. Over the years, I'd got quite clever about my bananas and I knew just where to cut them in order to have the best chance of a yes. At breakfast I would ask the question: does Simon love me? but meanwhile I was busy pondering the paradox of feeling that I hardly knew this person who last night had been so close to me that I had felt almost absorbed into his flesh.

"Oh, oh," cried Alice from the bed. "I'm coming, Bella. Stop tormenting me ... I'm waking up now, honestly." She swung her legs down on to the floor. "Oh, I hate the mornings! I hate getting up. I wish I could sleep some more." She shuffled off to the bathroom, moaning and shivering in the chilly half-light.

Bella's father and Marjorie were in the front row of the Parents' Gallery in Chapel that morning. Marjorie, whatever her other faults, was not a person who would miss an opportunity to impress the entire population of the school.

"You can't exactly accuse her," Bella whispered to me, up in the back row of the choir, "of not making an effort, can you? I mean, look at that fur hat and the quite unnecessarily sparkly diamonds in that brooch on her lapel."

"Maybe they're not diamonds. Maybe they're only glass."

Bella shook her head sadly. "They used to belong to my mother. They're real. The really ghastly part is, Daddy's plastered them all over her, or maybe she just helped herself and wheedled Daddy into agreeing to it afterward . . . but anyway, they're all my mother's jewels, and they should be mine—by rights, I mean. I bet my poor mother's turning in her grave."

"But do you like them? I think diamonds look a bit vulgar."

"That's not the point," said Bella. "Golly, look what Dorothy's just walked in with!"

I watched Simon sit down in the Staff pews next to Dorothy and felt confused and envious. Had Dorothy met him accidentally in the cloisters and had they wandered in together? Had she arranged to bring him? Why did it matter, anyway? Dorothy was my guardian, for goodness' sake. It was completely irrational to be jealous of her, particularly after last night. Nevertheless, I didn't like them sitting next to one another, nor did I like the way

Dorothy helped Simon find his place in the hymn book and prayer book as though he were a small child.

"You're turning slightly green," Bella murmured, "and I can't say I blame you. Why do you suppose Dorothy has touched up her lips with the dreaded, scorned, and totally reviled lipstick? Why is she wearing a dress I've only ever seen her wearing at Speech Day? Egad and gadzooks, madam, methinks you have a rival for your beau's affections!"

"Ssh! What rubbish! Dorothy and Simon? She's more than twenty years older than he is . . . It's disgusting. Ugh!"

"What about Phèdre?" Bella was relentless.

"What about her?"

"She was older than Hippolyte."

"But not forty-five," I said. "And anyway, Dorothy isn't Phèdre. You're just trying to worry me."

Bella giggled. "It's fun, that's why. You always believe everything and take everything so seriously. It was *you* he was kissing, wasn't it?"

I nodded. The day before, I had watched Dorothy and Simon leaving the labs together. At the time, I hadn't been in the least worried.

I don't think I even looked at them properly, but now, remembering it, I could see again the way the whole of Dorothy's body seemed to lean toward Simon's, almost to sway against him. Did she put her hand on his arm for a moment? I couldn't remember. What I did know was that when he had walked away, Dorothy had stood looking after him for a full minute. Was it only my imagination that made her gaze appear both loving and greedy? I couldn't decide. I looked at Simon, staring at the back of his head. If you stare at someone long enough and hard enough they will sometimes glance up at you, but it didn't work on this occasion. I was reduced to watching him and Dorothy, Bella's father and Marjorie, and all the assorted parents waiting to take their children out for the day. In the old days, we used to give people's mothers marks out of ten for their appearance and dress, but today I didn't even feel like doing that. I gazed morosely at the stained-glass windows full of angels with solid-looking arms and hefty legs standing around trying to seem mystical and transcendent. "They're about as ethereal, those angels," Bella remarked, "as the lacrosse team." Their plaited tresses hung down and

very conveniently hid any breasts they may
have had. They were draped in cunningly
arranged sheets and wore no shoes. You could
see their pinkish, feathery wings sticking up
over the edges of their shoulders. I sat there
wishing that Chapel were over.

We went to lunch at the Royal George Hotel
in Coleston. Parents, taking their daughters
out from Egerton Hall for the day, often came
to this dining room, decorated in pale green
and cream, with discreet little chandeliers dotted here and there over the high ceiling.
There were many Egerton Hall girls in their
navy blue regulation Sunday suits, looking like
a flock of dark birds pecking away at their tasty
lunches in the midst of the normal residents,
who were all uniformly ancient and seemed to
favor beige or sage green jersey and rows of
pearls. We, however, being Sixth Formers,
were allowed to wear our own clothes.

"Darling, do pass Alice the mint sauce,"
said Marjorie, "and Bella, dear, I should go
easy on the roast potatoes, if I were you."

"Pass the potatoes, please, Daddy," said
Bella, and she helped herself to four, deliber-
ately choosing the crispiest and oiliest.

Marjorie sighed audibly. "You young girls," she said, "just have no idea how easy it is to let your looks go. One has to be so careful."

"Bella doesn't," said Alice. "She eats a frightful lot, honestly, and it never makes any difference at all."

Alice's punishment for springing to Bella's defense was a pitying smile from Marjorie. She said, "You, Alice dear, look very thin indeed to me. Positively unwell. Are you sure you're getting enough vitamins?"

"Oh, yes, thank you," said Alice. "I'm much stronger than I look, really."

"Well, you must make sure that Bella shares her fruit with you. I've given her simply bags and bags of apples, so do have some, and please, Alice and Megan, make sure that Bella has apples rather than those dreadful Mars bars to which she's addicted. We don't want her turning spotty, now do we?"

"No danger of that," said Bella's father, who up till now had been silently munching through his lamb. "Skin like untrodden snow, Bella's got. Always has had. Always will have."

Marjorie flashed him a look of pure hatred and her mouth tightened. She changed the subject at once.

"And how have you all got on with the examinations?" she said.

Before leaving the hotel for the cinema, we went to the Ladies, Alice and Bella and I, to repair our makeup and fiddle with our hair and enjoy the luxury of thick pink carpets, bowls of plastic flowers, and mirrors lit with pink lamps.

"I used to hate going out in uniform," said Bella, "when we were in the Lower School. I hated everyone in Coleston knowing we were from Egerton Hall."

"It's all right for you," I said. "Your home clothes are lovely. Mine are all . . . I don't know . . . wrong somehow. I'd rather be wearing a uniform. Then people say: Oh, she looks like that because of the uniform, and they imagine how nice you'd look in real clothes."

"You need someone to go with you when you're trying on," said Bella.

"I go with Dorothy, generally," I said.

"And it shows," said Bella.

"Don't be beastly," said Alice. "Megan can't help it. And anyway, she always looks nice."

"I'm not beastly, Alice," said Bella. "I know Megan looks nice, but for your party, for instance . . . well, she's going to need something special and I think it'd be better if she let me or you choose it, and not Dorothy."

"The party's not till June," I said. "I can't think why you're so worried about it in January. It's only Alice who's going to be the Belle of the Ball, and who's had silkworms in China nibbling themselves into a frenzy for years."

Alice laughed. "It's silk and lace, my dress, and the only reason you know about it is because Aunt Ivy goes on about everything so much. She's making it, so of course, she has to keep having these conferences with Aunt Lily, who designed it, and we keep having to have these fittings."

"Is the dreaded Violette coming to the party?" I asked. "I'd love to meet her, after all your tales."

"After the fuss she caused at my christening," said Alice, "I don't think they'd like to risk *not* inviting her."

"Not inviting whom where, darlings?" trilled Marjorie, pushing herself into the room with a majestic swing of the pink door.

"Nothing, Marjorie," Bella sang out as she swept from the room. "Don't pick up any butts!"

Alice followed her. Marjorie turned to me and wrinkled her nose slightly. A true grimace was hard for her. It would have made too many creases in her smooth, beige foundation.

"I can't think where Bella picks up such language," she said to me. "We pay enough to send her to that blasted school, Heaven knows, and then it's 'butts' all over the place!" She shuddered delicately and turned up the fur collar of her suit.

"We all say things like that, Mrs. Lavanne," I said to placate her. "Much worse things than that, sometimes."

Marjorie appeared to have lost interest in Bella and in our conversation. She was staring into the mirror as if mesmerized by her own reflection, pulling with a dainty finger at the skin under her eyes.

"This *is* a kind mirror," she smiled. "I expect it must be the pink lights. I wonder whether I shouldn't put some in at home. What do you think, Megan? Don't you think it's effective? I can hardly see the crow's-feet at all, can you?"

I bent down so that our faces were in the mirror together.

"What are crow's-feet?" I asked.

"The little lines . . . wrinkles around the eyes one gets as one gets older. Haven't you heard of them before?"

"No, no, never. But cheer up," I said. "I can't see any, anyway." I was lying, of course, but you couldn't tell unpleasant truths to someone who'd just bought you a really delicious lunch. I couldn't have lied very convincingly, however, because Marjorie said not a word. Dark furrows appeared on her brow, and you could almost see the anger rising from every line of her body, like steam. I had never met anyone who was so anxious about their appearance. Every sign of age she noticed seemed to make her more and more desperate. She opened her crocodile-skin handbag and began a ferocious attack on her mouth with a lipstick whose color was uncomfortably like the scarlet of freshly spilled blood.

We always had to be back at school in time for Evensong. Between the end of Evensong and bedtime on Sunday night, there were a couple of hours that were a kind of limbo, an emptiness when it seemed to all of us that one week had ended and the next had not yet properly begun. It was a time I always thought of as sad, probably because so many people had seen their parents during the day and felt homesick on Sunday nights. There was always, in the

Junior House anyway, more cheering up to do on Sunday nights than at any other time.

"I'm never sad on Sunday nights," said Bella. "I love coming back from going out with Her. It's no hardship at all."

For the Sixth Form, after Evensong was when we all crowded into the S.C.R. together. Prefects left their studies and we all lolled about, devouring the goodies devoted sets of parents had given us, and which were meant to last us until the next time we saw them. Pippa Grey was toasting a crumpet in front of the gas fire, having previously impaled it on her compass, and Marion Tipton was doing her best to divide a Fuller's walnut cake into seven pieces.

"I don't see why you can't have a bit, Sally," she said. "Then it'll be eight pieces and much easier to cut."

"Because I'm slimming."

"Well, why don't I cut a piece for you and then you can give it to someone else?"

"No." Sally was adamant. "If you cut it, I shall want it. If there are only seven bits there anyway, then I can say there's not enough for me and that's that."

Marion sighed and continued to measure and calculate.

"Here, Sal," said Bella from the depths of the armchair into which she had slumped, "have an apple. Marjorie's best, I promise you, and all homegrown. They look positively slimming, don't they?"

She took one out of a paper bag that lay beside the chair and held it up for everyone to see.

"In fact," she said, "it looks so marvelous that I think I shall have one, too."

"Does that mean," said Marion, "that I can cut this blasted thing into six?"

"No, you can't," Bella said. "So there. I shall have both. Cake first and apple later."

"There you are, then," said Marion, "and if anyone feels hard done by, then I'm sorry. That's the best I can do."

After the cake had been finished, after every morsel of gossip from the day had been thoroughly chewed over, after a few frantic searches for work that was due to be given in the next day, and a major hunt behind desks and sofas for Rowena Menzies's copy of *Renny's Daughter*, without which she refused to go to bed, Alice, Bella, and I began the long trudge up to the Tower Room. Bella had the apple in her hand.

"The question is," she said, "can I wait till I

get into bed to eat this, or is it too tempting? Shall I succumb like Eve? Look how red and shiny it is! I wonder if it *is* plastic? I wouldn't put anything past Marjorie."

She opened her mouth wide and took a huge bite out of the apple. The next moment, she was choking. Alice noticed first.

"Megan! Look, Bella's choking . . . oh, goodness, Megan. What shall we do?"

Luckily, we were almost at the landing where Matron had her room. I shouted at Alice, "Quick! Get Matron. Tell her it's urgent."

Alice flew up the stairs. Bella's eyes had grown enormous in her face, and her arms were flailing about. I tried everything I could think of: banging her on her shoulder, holding her arms above her head . . . and all the time she was growing blue under my very eyes. It seemed like years till Matron arrived, although it couldn't have been more than a few seconds. I was so relieved to see her, I hardly noticed what she did, but she seemed to give Bella a punch in the chest. Whatever it was, it worked. A lump of apple the size of a golf ball flew out of Bella's mouth, and she sank down on to the stairs like a rag doll. Matron put her arms around her.

"There," she said. "That's better. Now, Alice, stop crying at once. You and Megan behaved very sensibly. It was your speed, Alice, that quite probably saved Bella's life."

"I'd never have thought to get you," sobbed Alice, "if Megan hadn't told me to."

"Quite so," said Matron. "Well done, Megan. And you, young lady"—she turned to look down at Bella—"will have learned to eat a trifle more daintily. How are you feeling?"

"Fine," Bella tried to say, but her voice had almost entirely disappeared.

"I think that apple must have hurt your throat. I shall drive you to the San, and then Dr. Murray can have a look at you tomorrow. Does your throat hurt?"

Bella nodded.

"I thought so," said Matron. "Megan, you and Alice go into my sitting room and make yourselves a cup of cocoa before bed. You both deserve it. You can go and visit Bella tomorrow. Come on, now, child."

Bella tottered to her feet. She and Matron staggered downstairs together.

In Matron's room, over the cocoa, Alice said, "She could have died, Megan, couldn't she?"

"It'd take a lot more than a bit of apple to kill Bella," I said.

"But she could have, couldn't she?"

"I suppose so. But she didn't. So shut up about dying and drink your cocoa."

We drank in silence and then went up to the Tower Room together.

LONDON *April 20, 1962*

Sometimes, when I wake up, you've gone. It's not your fault of course, because you have to travel right across London to get to your lab in time for 8:45. I like to lie in bed late, though. It's the only thing about Egerton Hall that I really don't miss—that hideous seven o'clock bell. Oh, I was used to it, of course I was, and never quite like Alice, having to be physically pulled by the hair from a deep, deep sleep, but still, I shudder to remember the horror of waking up on cold dark mornings, when the lino was like a sheet of ice, and there was frost on the inside of our windows. One tiny radiator that was only ever lukewarm was all we had: no gas fires, naturally. Was it any wonder that we used to put most of our clothes on under the blankets?

Here, the gas fire is always already on when I wake up. You know how much I like its apricot glow. There's sometimes a note on the table: "Late back tonight on acct. important

meeting. Love, S." or "Could you get some
toothpaste—Macleans pref." It's a far cry, isn't
it, from Keats to Fanny Brawn in July 1819: "I
will imagine you Venus tonight, and pray,
pray, pray to your star like a heathen." Still,
the first time I ever saw your handwriting on a
piece of paper, I nearly died of bliss. Just the
shapes of the letters on the page, the idea of
your hand, your pen, making my own name
appear in black on all that white—oh, it was
wonderful! And at the time I had no quarrel
with the content, either. You wanted to see me
again. You mentioned a time, and I knew I
would be there. You had taken the trouble to
find out (how? whom did you ask? Fiona?)
when I was free, and I knew how I was going
to spend the time between the moment of
finding your note (Sunday night) and Wednesday evening at five o'clock. I was going to
press your small, neat words close to my heart,
fold them up and tuck them into my bra, so
that I could at least be touching something *you*
had written. I was going to take your note out
twenty times a day and look at it. Its words
would become an enchantment, a rune. What
did it matter to me that you weren't Keats?
You were you: a scientist and not a poet. I was
writing enough poetry for both of us, great

unstoppable spurts of the stuff. I felt as though a lid had been taken off a steaming cauldron. I have to admit, though, that maybe Dorothy was right, after all. Looking at it now, I see that most of it *is* a morass of sentimentality, and all of it is so purple that you could use it on cut knees instead of gentian violet.

Alice and I went to see Bella in the San on Monday at lunchtime.

"I'm a fraud," she said. "There's nothing whatsoever wrong with me. I'm just lying here being spoiled."

"But you nearly died, Bella," Alice wailed.

"Oh, Alice, do stop being so melodramatic. I'm not dead, am I? That's the point. It's useless to say: 'You nearly died.' I mean, we don't know how near death we are at any time, do we?"

Alice thought about this. I said, "Oh, shut up about death, you two. Alice, you *do* keep going on about it. I've got something much more interesting to show you. Look."

I fished inside my blouse and took a note out of my bra.

"What on earth is that and why are you keeping it there?" Bella asked.

"Because it's precious and it's private. It's from Simon."

Bella read it.

"Gadzooks, sirrah," she giggled, "an assignation! How smashing! Wednesday at five . . . uhm . . . I think I'm just going to creep up to the Tower Room and . . ."

"Don't you dare, Bella," I shouted. "Oh, you wouldn't, would you? Oh, please, please don't spoil it."

"'Course I won't. I might even station myself on the landing below and keep *cave*. Never let it be said that Bella Lavanne stopped the course of true love running smooth . . . and in return you'll lie like mad for me on the seventeenth."

"I suppose so," I sighed. "But look at the note. Don't you think it's blissful?"

"I don't know that I'd necessarily call 'Dear Megan, How about Wednesday at five, Tower Room? Love, Simon.' blissful."

"But he said 'love.' And 'dear.' 'Dear Megan' . . . I mean, he didn't have to put my name at all, or 'Love, Simon' if it comes to that."

"And," said Alice, "he went to the trouble of finding out when she was free. And he must have taken a risk coming right up to the Tower Room and putting it on her chest of drawers. The window was shut, so he couldn't use the scaffolding."

"I'm bored with this conversation," said Bella. "Guess who's in the San with me. You'll never guess."

"Tell us," I said.

"Miss van der Leyden. Sister told me."

"What's the matter with her?" I said. "She's never ill."

"I don't know."

"I'll go and ask Sister," I said, "if I can visit her before we go back to afternoon school."

Sister was exactly like a series of cottage loaves enclosed in a starched, white overall. She had a round face topped with a round, gray bun, and a mound-shaped bosom that seemed stuck to the front of her body. Her cheeks were pink and shiny. She wore a watch pinned to her breast pocket, and it bounced around as she walked, sometimes bumping into a thermometer in a silver case.

"Miss van der Leyden," she told me, "simply needs to rest. She's not been feeling quite herself lately."

"May I say hello to her? Just for a second?"

"Creep in, dear, and see if she's awake. I don't want you waking her up, mind you ... not if she's asleep. She's in Room Four, up the stairs and to the left."

I opened Miss van der Leyden's door as quietly as I could. At first I thought she must be dead, because her hands were folded on the counterpane, her head was lolling, and her mouth gaped open. Then she let out a small, snoring kind of breath, and I jumped back. Her fingers, thickened, knotted, and twisted like the hidden roots of trees, lay so still. I'd never seen them idle before. Always Miss van der Leyden was making something: little four-ply cardigans for other people's babies and gossamer lace mats to sit under the perfume bottles on the dressing tables of prettier women. I closed the door, hoping that I hadn't disturbed her. Perhaps, I thought, I'll come and visit her tomorrow ... but I knew I wouldn't. I would leave it until she was back in her little room at the top of Junior House. Seeing her lying there frightened me. I remembered the curtain of the room blowing a little in the draught and thought it could have been a corner of the wings of the Angel of Death ... Haven't I said I'm of a fanciful turn of mind? I put my hand on my heart to feel the crackling of Simon's note and promptly forgot about everything else. If the Four Horsemen of the Apocalypse had galloped into the San on skeleton mounts, I wouldn't even have seen them.

LONDON *April 22, 1962*

I never did return to the San to visit Miss van der Leyden. Bella came back into school that evening, and in the fever of waiting for Wednesday and our second meeting, I forgot all about her. Now she is in the hospital in Coleston and it nags at me that I can't go and visit her every week. Nobody has said what's the matter with her, but she must be quite old, and I can't help feeling she may have something terrible and be dying of it. Alice goes, I know, and I feel about this a mixture of relief and resentment, even jealousy. Miss van der Leyden has always had a special place in her heart for Alice, because Alice, of all of us, was the child who knew immediately and instinctively how to hold her knitting needles, how to make that length of wool running between her fingers twist effortlessly into smooth expanses of fabric and intricate patterns. The rest of us produced tatty, uneven pieces of stocking stitch, full of holes and with edges that went in and out like rocky coastlines. Mine was one of the worst in the whole class. Only Alice, at the end of a term, had made a little yellow matinée jacket, complete with ribbon trimmings. Golden hands, Miss van der Leyden said she had, and it was true.

"*Tenez, mes enfants,*" she would say, "the back of Alice's embroideries is as neat as the front, do you see?" She would hold up the work to show us.

"The front of my embroidery," said Bella under her breath, "is just as messy as the back. Isn't that the same thing?"

"You know it isn't, stupid," I said, trying not to laugh.

Bella, Alice had written to me, refused to go to the hospital "and so I go on my own, but I hate hospitals. They smell so awful, and everyone looks so ghastly, especially Miss v.d.L. Her face is quite gray. I wish you were here to come with me."

Whatever happens, whatever I decide to do, one thing is certain: I shall have to visit Miss van der Leyden in the hospital. I don't want her to think I've forgotten about her. Also, it's not fair that Alice should have to keep going to a place she hates all on her own. I wish sometimes that Alice were not such a good letter writer. She's had so much practice. Of the three of us, she was the one who was always writing letters to this aunt or that, sending cards to cousins, and during the last few weeks, writing letters to Jean-Luc.

This had become almost a daily event, and it was lucky for me that it had. Alice swapped with me and took prep in the J.P.R., happily attending to her correspondence while I climbed the stairs to the Tower Room and waited for you.

At half past five, I was sitting on my bed and there was no sign of Simon. I went over to the window and looked out, my heart still beating very fast from the terror of creeping up all those stairs as quietly as I could and trying at the same time to look nonchalant. I had worked out a plausible story in case anyone (Matron, Miss Doolittle) was unexpectedly patrolling the corridors: I just had to run up and fetch my Spanish Lit file, which I'd stupidly left in the Tower Room. But I didn't meet anyone. As Saint John of the Cross puts it in his poem, the whole house was hushed, but my heart sounded as loud as a drum in my own ears. I left the window and glanced around the room to make sure that everything was tidy. Absurd notions filled my head: I should have brought up something to eat ... been able to offer Simon a cup of tea ... and then, quite suddenly, he was there, tapping on the glass of the window. I went over and let him in.

"Hello," he said. "Frightfully sorry to be so late, but I had to wait until the coast was clear ..."

"It's all right," I said, and then couldn't think what to say next. I didn't know how to act, how to be. I didn't know where to put my hands, or what happened next. My mouth felt dry.

"Are you glad I'm here?" Simon said, sitting down on Bella's bed.

"Oh, yes," I said, and because I felt I had to say something, almost anything else, I added, "I'm just a bit nervous. I mean I *was*, coming upstairs during prep. What if we're caught?"

"We won't be caught. Everyone's busy. No one's going to come looking for you now, or me, come to that. Oh, Megan, don't look so terrified! Come over here and sit by me. Let me loosen your hair again. I love to touch it, to smell it. Have you forgotten the last time?"

I shook my head, meaning "no," because I simply did not trust myself to speak. I was sure that if I so much as opened my mouth, words of love would pour out of it and spill into the air before I could stop them. I went silently to sit beside Simon, and he put his arms around me and kissed me and undid my plait, and I felt as though every part of me were also being unraveled: as though my body had turned into liquid, rushing gold.

It seems that in kissing you don't need an awful lot of practice before you become rather good at it, and not only good at it, but also able to sort out in your head the different kinds of kisses, the feelings behind them. Last time, maybe because it was the first time for me, everything was trembling, tentative, shivery. My legs felt weak, I remembered, and my head swam. Now, I could feel an urgency, a force running through both our bodies like a fever, a need to be close, to merge, to sink one into the other. I could feel Simon's hands undoing the buttons on my school blouse.

"No, please . . . please don't," I said.

"But why not? Don't you want me to? I want to see you . . ."

"No. Not here."

"But there *is* nowhere else. Please, Megan."

"No, I'd feel funny. I couldn't."

Simon smiled. "I'm rushing you. I'm sorry. I really am sorry. I won't rush you again. Come and kiss me and we'll forget about it."

So I went and I kissed him and maybe he forgot about it, but I didn't. I felt torn in half. Part of me wanted him to touch me and wanted to touch him. What would his back be like? His legs? I could hardly bear to imagine how his skin would feel. Another part of me said: But you hardly know him . . . you've hardly spoken. You know nothing about him. I pulled away from him in the end and tried to speak, tried to have a conversation, but it was difficult to concentrate in between kisses. He left after an hour, and I lay on the bed and waited for the bell to call me to supper.

That night, Bella interrogated me.

"Don't you two ever talk at all? Did you find out anything at all about him?"

"He's got two sisters. His mother is a widow. They live in Brighton. He met Dorothy at some scientific party. He's only helping out because he's waiting to start a job in some school in London next term."

"Did you ask him about Fiona?" Bella wanted to know.

"What about her?"

"Well, is he kissing her as well? You on Mondays, Wednesdays, and Fridays, and her on Tuesdays, Thursdays, and Saturdays, rather like the Bath Rota. Maybe he has to fit in Dorothy as well. They do so often seem to be having a chinwag and a smile together. Almost whenever one sees them."

"Simon's very polite," I said. "He has to be polite to Dorothy."

"Not that polite, I shouldn't have thought."

"Oh, Bella, shut up! You are awful!" Alice said. "He couldn't possibly be doing something like that. No one could."

"Don't be so naive." Bella laughed. "He could easily. I should think it would be very easy for him."

"I'm sure he isn't," I said, although I wasn't as sure as I tried to sound. "I mean, he kisses me so . . . well, so very passionately. I'm sure he loves me. I'm sure he wouldn't be kissing someone else." My voice trailed away. Suddenly I was full of doubts, worries that hadn't been there before.

"Has he said he loves you?" Alice wanted to know.

"No, but that doesn't mean anything. I haven't said I love him."

"*Do* you love him?" Bella asked.

"Oh, yes, I'd do anything for him. Anything at all."

"You wouldn't even let him touch your breasts," said Bella. "You've just told us."

"Well, I was frightened. I wanted him to, really, but I didn't dare. It seemed so strange, all that sort of thing happening up here, in this room. I mean, what if someone came in? There isn't even a lock on the door."

"Cowardy, cowardy, cowardy custard!" Bella grinned. "He'll have his wicked way with you before long, though. Bet you anything."

"Do you *have* to call it that?" I was suddenly irritated, annoyed at Bella for reducing feelings that were nearly overwhelming me to the status of something from a cheap romance. "I love him. Maybe you've never been in love and can't understand how I feel."

"Oh, sorry I spoke!" said Bella. "I shall treat your precious Love with the respect it deserves in the future, never fear."

"Oh, for goodness' sake," said Alice, who hated any kind of row and was always smoothing over situations like this, "don't start fighting over nothing. Go to sleep, both of you."

Bella sighed. "I didn't mean to laugh at you, you know, Megan, but you shouldn't take everything so seriously. Just because he's the first, doesn't necessarily mean he'll be the last. He'll be gone in a few weeks and you'll probably never see him again."

"Oh, don't say that, Bella," Alice groaned. "You're making Megan sad all over again."

"No, she's not," I said, "it's OK. I'm sure she's right, Alice, and I shouldn't make so much of it. As a matter of fact, that's probably exactly what'll happen at the end of term: I'll stay and he'll go and that will probably be that. Actually, I don't know what he sees in me, if you really want to know."

"It's your sterling character," said Bella. "Your integrity, honesty, etc., etc. Or your brains."

"Don't be stupid," I said. "I don't think people get attracted by sterling qualities."

"Maybe he thinks you're pretty," Alice suggested.

"But I'm not," I said. "Not especially."

"There must be something about you," said Bella, "that appeals to him. Something physical that drives him wild with desire. Something deep and secret that no one will ever know, which thrills him to the core . . ."

"What a lot of rot you do talk, Bella," I said

lightly, but I smiled into the darkness, thinking of the way Simon's hands had trembled in
my hair, of how he had covered his face with
its strands, twined it in his fingers, and
breathed endearments into it. I felt weak
thinking these thoughts. I lifted the plaited
weight of it and felt the silkiness and intricacy
of the braid in my hand like a smooth rope.

The others fell asleep shortly after this conversation, but I stayed awake, imagining a
life in which Simon and I would share a house
that looked very much like Alice's. Alice's parents had a wide, wide bed covered with a
maroon satin counterpane. I closed my eyes
and imagined myself and Simon in such a
place, lying on those crisp white sheets with
our bodies entwined. I must have fallen asleep
in the end.

Perhaps because of what Bella had said, I
seemed to see Simon and Fiona together a
great deal during the next couple of weeks. It
wasn't that he had stopped coming to the
Tower Room. Those meetings had continued
and increased in frequency, so that by the
middle of February, I almost knew what it was
like to live two totally separate lives. In one, I

was a prefect, a schoolgirl. I did my duties,
supervised Junior prep, studied for my lessons,
took part in class discussions, sat around in the
study listening to Radio Lux, went to Chapel,
sang in the choir, gossiped with my friends.
No one seeing me could have guessed that
almost every other day, as if by a kind of
magic, I would change, transform myself as I
went up that staircase to meet Simon, and that
in the Tower Room I would lose myself in
sensations, feelings, agonies of love and desire.
For hours, we lay on the bed (my bed . . . I
made sure of that) and explored one another. I
thought each time that I would faint away
from the strength of my love, that it would,
eventually, drown me, carry me away completely like a wave. I hadn't, as Bella rather
crudely put it, "gone all the way," but that was
because I was frightened, terrified of becom-
ing pregnant. Still, each time we met, I feared
that this would be the time that I wouldn't be
able to resist . . . I would allow myself to be
engulfed by love and lose all grasp of common
sense. But there was the matter of Fiona to be
dealt with. One evening, I asked him directly,
"Are you meeting Fiona Mackenzie like this,
Simon?"

He threw back his head and laughed so much I had to cover his mouth with my hand because he was making such a noise.

"Don't be silly, Megan, honestly! It's a full-time job clambering up here all the time, I can tell you."

"Well, no one makes you," I said huffily. "You don't *have* to come."

"But I *want* to, can't you understand? I'm in a complete tizz over you, Megan, you must know that. I can't bloody think straight for dreaming about you all the time. Can't you feel how much I want you, Megan, when we're together like this, in this room? Fiona Mackenzie's nothing, truly. It's hard to avoid her, that's all. She's in the labs all the time, isn't she? I don't see any point in being unfriendly." He beamed at me, pleased with himself.

I believed him. I had to believe him and needed to believe him. Nevertheless, late that night I lay in bed and went over his words. Words are very important to me. They mean something. They carry associations. "I'm in a complete tizz over you" somehow didn't have the force or the weight of "I love you." They seemed frivolous, purely physical. "Can't you feel how much I want you?" Yes, that was exactly what I *could* feel, but it was more than that I wanted. I made a silent resolution: if Simon ever says it, sincerely and truly, if he ever says the words "I love you" and really means them, I will let him make love to me. If he says them, those syllables will be an open sesame, an enchanted password.

The next day, Dorothy met me in the corridor and stopped to talk.

"I've been meaning to send for you, dear," she said. "It has been such a long time since we've had a good chat. I was very pleased with your examination results, by the bye."

"Thank you," I said. I thought to myself: Exams! What ages ago they were, and how trivial and silly they now seem compared with what I'm feeling. I had almost forgotten I'd done well ... and why did Dorothy have to say "by the bye" when everyone else in the world said "by the way"? Dorothy continued, "I'm having a small tea party on Saturday, in my room. Just Simon ... Simon Findlay, I mean, of course, and you and Fiona Mackenzie. Do come, dear."

"That'll be very nice, Dorothy. Thanks tons. I have to go to French now. See you on Saturday."

Was there a tiny flutter in Dorothy's voice as she said Simon's name, or was I imagining it? I rushed along School Corridor, cursing the malign fate that had made Fiona good at science. Just my luck. How was I going to be able to eat sandwiches and drink tea in the same room with Fiona, Simon, and Dorothy? I was meeting Simon on Friday night. My neck and arms would be bruised from his kisses, and I'd have to sit there making polite conversation. . . . Oh, it would be dreadful!

That afternoon, Bella came into the study just as Alice and I were settling down to our work.

"Is Marion not here?" she said. "Goody goody. I can use her desk. The Walker creature is slowly killing me, and besides, we have to have a planning discussion."

"What are we planning?" I said. "You are a nuisance, Bella, honestly you are. How am I ever going to finish this essay and give it in by suppertime?"

"It won't take long and then I'll shut up, I promise. Only I want to arrange the Drop. I think that's what it's called."

"I don't know about you, Megan," said Alice, "but I haven't the foggiest idea what's going on. What's a drop? What are we planning?"

"Oh, Alice, don't be so feeble!" said Bella. "You know jolly well that I've thought of nothing else for weeks. Saturday is the day I'm climbing down the scaffolding and doing my singing with Pete and the band. You must remember."

"Yes, I do now," said Alice. "Of course I do." She sighed. "It's just that I hate the idea of it so much—you climbing down in the dark and running through the forest . . . I mean the forest, Bella, and at night!" Alice shivered. "I'd be petrified. I would, truly. And that's not to mention worrying about getting caught and getting expelled. I do wish you wouldn't go."

"But I've got to, can't you see that? I've been living for it. You just haven't a clue how marvelous, how splendiferously gorgeous it feels to be up there, with everyone looking at you and listening to you and your voice, your music just floating out of your mouth and over their heads like a . . . like a beautiful white bird."

"I think I'd faint," said Alice. "I think you're fantastically brave. I wouldn't do it for anything. It's almost more terrifying than the forest at night."

Bella laughed. "It's not a forest, Alice, it's a wood, and anyway, where's your *Malory Towers* spirit, gals? Don't you remember Alicia and Darrell Rivers? Whatever would they think if they saw you trembling at the thought of an adventure? This is a real-life, school story kind of adventure, and all I'm asking is a tiny bit of help from you, my chums, and you're turning into . . . into drips, that's what."

"It's all right, Bella," I said. "We'll help you, of course we will. What do you want us to do?"

"The main thing is, could you put my party clothes somewhere safe, just inside the forest? There's that little shed. You know . . . you go up behind the San and there it is: hardly in the forest at all, really. I mean, I'd do it myself, only I don't want to leave my stuff there too long, and on Friday I'm doing netball at Games time and lessons all afternoon, then I'm taking prep. I'd leave it till Saturday, but you've got Dorothy's tea party, Megan, and Alice, you're going on this Art Gallery outing, aren't you? So it's got to be Friday. You two can wander over to the San on your walk, can't you? Please?"

"I suppose so," I said. "But what on earth are you going to put your clothes in?"

Bella smiled triumphantly. "My sack, of course."

Sacks were the large shopping bag–shaped things that we all carried our books around in. They were tough, made of a canvas that was as thick as tarpaulin, and held an enormous amount.

"You should take my sack," said Alice. "Mine hasn't got any writing on it at all. Even my name tape's fallen off. If anyone finds yours, they'll know immediately whose it is." Bella's sack had slogans, names, and huge red hearts drawn in ballpoint pen all over it. She had written "Bella Lavanne" in italic capitals and green ink down one side, had stated that she loved Buddy Holly, Elvis Presley, The Everly Brothers, Jerry Lee Lewis, Connie Francis, and a few other people whose names had been rained on and had run into blue and red messes here and there.

"Good thinking, old sport," she said to Alice. "You'll get quite good at all this adventure stuff in the end. So, you'll do it, will you?"

"I suppose so," I said. "What are you wearing?"

"My red circular skirt and high heels. And I've got a pair of black stockings. And I thought I'd wear (if you'll be an absolute angel and lend it to me) your black cardigan. I'll wear it with the buttons down the back, of course."

"Where's Pete meeting you?" Alice asked. "Why don't you ask him to come to the hut?"

"Too late now," Bella said, "and anyway, I don't mind about the forest at night. I shall have my flashlight and it's only five minutes' walk to the road. I'll be fine."

"Just be careful," I said. "You are taking a risk, you know. What if you're caught?"

Bella burst out laughing. "I like that! You're a fine one to talk about risk! All that spooning in the Tower Room. Asking for trouble, I call that."

I think I blushed. Then Marion came back from a lesson, and we changed the subject. Bella sat down in between the desks, and I turned to my essay, wondering how I was going to write intelligently about the role of fate in the short stories of Guy de Maupassant in the half hour left before supper.

Spooning in the Tower Room: that's what Bella called it. That's, I suppose, what it was, only I used to think of it so differently. I made the room, in my mind, into an enchanted place, not part of the real world at all. And we changed, too, Simon and I. I felt it every time

I went up the stairs, every time I heard his movements on the scaffolding outside the window. We were transformed into more beautiful, more amusing, altogether better people. Our silliest remarks and giggles became brilliantly witty, our most trivial words profound and moving, and when we spoke of the future, of what our lives would be like, it was as though we were describing heaven, as though our futures were very distant from us, and not in any way connected to the present. The whole of time and the world and everything in it shrank each time we met until it was us, us, us, and nothing but us existed.

"I feel," said Alice on Friday afternoon, as we walked along the path toward the San and the forest, "like a criminal."

"I know," I answered. "Me, too." I was carrying Alice's sack full of Bella's stuff hidden (I hoped) under my cloak. "I feel as if I'm carrying a body . . . going to bury it somewhere."

"Don't," Alice shivered. "I can't bear the forest."

"But why ever not? It's only trees, when you come right down to it. No animals, apart from the odd rabbit, I'm sure. Nothing to be scared of, really."

"I know," said Alice. "I know that *really* but . . . well, I had this book when I was little. I can't even remember what the story was. It could have been 'Red Riding Hood,' I suppose, but the pictures were horrible: these tree trunks that had human faces and all the branches like arms reaching out and twig fingers at the ends . . . ugh. And it's worse in winter when there are no leaves."

"But they were only pictures in a story. You shouldn't let your imagination run away with you. You'll be saying this old wooden hut is like the witch's sugar house in 'Hansel and Gretel' in a minute."

Alice giggled. "Nonsense, Megan! It's just an old gardening shed. It's where Mr. Carter keeps the roller for the cricket pitches and the lawn mower and things. Now *you're* being silly."

"I know I am," I said, as we put Bella's clothes in the appointed spot just inside the door. I glanced back at the shed as we walked away from it. The two small windows looked like eyes, the ramshackle roof was a hat, the door separating the windows, a nose, and there was even a scratch in the battered paintwork of the door just where the mouth should be on a face . . . and I was daring to accuse Alice of having too much imagination.

"Come on," I said, "it's nearly time for prep."

Alice nodded, and we hurried away, and the trees vanished behind us as twilight gathered in their branches. Alice may still have been worrying about Bella for all I knew. My mind had run ahead of me, and I was already halfway up the stairs to the Tower Room, hardly able to catch my breath, longing for the moment when Simon's face would appear at the window.

"Do have another slice of Battenburg, Simon dear," said Dorothy. "And you, too, of course, Megan and Fiona."

Dorothy was beaming. I don't think I had ever seen her beam before. Her cheeks were either very flushed or (amazing thought!) she had put on some rouge. It must have been for Simon's benefit. Her behavior could only be called "flirtatious," and I found this new, strange Dorothy that I had never seen before very embarrassing, even worrying. Dorothy, after all, was my guardian, and I had no desire for Simon to think she was a fool.

So far, the party had gone as well as I could have expected. Fiona had batted her eyelashes, just as I had warned Simon she would when I was lying in his arms last night.

"Shut up about Fiona. I'm not interested in Fiona . . . it's you. Oh, Megan, come away with me! We could live together all the time and never have to be apart, not for a minute, and never have to worry all the time about being found out, and I could use the stairs instead of climbing up walls like a spider . . . Come on, leave all this . . . let's run away. Now."

I'd laughed. "Don't be silly," I'd said. "I've got my A-levels."

"Gosh, you're unromantic . . . come here . . ."

I thought about all this while the tea party was going on. Dorothy had provided scones and cucumber sandwiches and shortbread and Battenburg cake, which I hated more because of its nasty coloring than because of its taste. The conversation had covered such thrilling topics as The Arts versus The Sciences (in which I was outnumbered three to one), single-sex schools versus coeducational establishments, the forthcoming lacrosse match against Benenden (well, all right, Fiona was Captain of Games) and, of course, A-levels.

"I have great hopes for Megan," Dorothy said in tones that could only be described as "skittish." "I know I'm only your guardian, dear, but I do have a mother's feelings in this.

Megan's mother, you see"—she turned to Simon—"entrusted the child to me before she died." Simon nodded solemnly. Dorothy continued, "It is my responsibility to see that she . . . fulfills herself. Lives up to her potential. She has done rather well in these Mock Examinations."

"Yes, I know," said Simon. "They were jolly good marks, weren't they?" He smiled happily at Dorothy. I froze in my chair and clutched my saucer so hard that I nearly spilled Earl Grey all over Dorothy's pale blue carpet. Oh, Simon, I thought, after what I told you last night about watching your tongue you have to go and make a mistake like that! I was considering spilling the tea on purpose and creating a diversion, but it was too late. Dorothy, exact, methodical, and sharp, wasn't going to miss something like this. Her fluttery, girlish demeanor disappeared into thin air.

"How do you know what Megan's marks were, Simon?" she said, and each word as it emerged from her mouth hung in the air like an icicle. Simon went on nonchalantly, munching his Battenburg.

"You told me, Dorothy, don't you remember?" he said and flashed Dorothy a smile of such brilliance that you could almost see her thaw. The stiffness that had set in around her mouth and neck dissolved in the warmth. She said, "Did I? I *am* a forgetful creature! Getting quite absentminded in my old age . . ."

Simon knew his cue. "Absentminded, perhaps," he twinkled, "but old, never."

Dorothy forgot about me, about Fiona, about her tea party, and simpered. That was the only word to describe what she was doing. I was more relieved than I can say when the tea party was over. I felt I'd been holding my breath underwater for a long, long time. Fiona walked down School Corridor with me.

"I call it absolutely revolting!" she said. "She's old enough to be his mother."

"She *was* being a bit silly," I agreed weakly.

"Silly? I call it worse than that. Did you see how she was pawing him? Walking around behind his chair and resting her hand on his shoulder, pulling his arm through hers as she walked to the door with us . . . patting his *cheek*, for goodness' sake . . . oh, just playfully, of course. But I ask you, you're her child, practically, so you know what I mean. When is Dorothy ever playful?"

"No, she isn't. She isn't ever."

"She is now. You should just see her in the labs. Honestly, she's a laughingstock! 'Simon, could you come here a second,' or 'Simon, I wonder whether you'd mind...' Seriously, she doesn't leave him alone for five minutes. It's pathetic, that's what it is. Got to dash now, though, Megan. See you later." Fiona ran down Browning House's Study Passage before I could ask her the really important question: how did Simon behave when Dorothy was "being pathetic"? I remembered looking at them in Chapel, coming out of the labs, walking along School Corridor. I paused now, wondering why Simon hadn't left Dorothy's room at the same time that Fiona and I did, my heart contracting at the thought of the two of them alone together.

Alice and I found it harder than usual to go to sleep that night. We'd arranged that Bella should tap on the window three times when she got back, and I would wake up and let her in. The alternative was not to be contemplated in this weather: sleeping with the window open till morning. We would have been frost-bitten by dawn.

"I wonder what she's doing now," Alice said at about midnight.

"Bopping...jiving...whatever they call it...with Pete or one of the others. Or maybe it's what she calls 'her spot': the bit where she gets up and sings."

"I hope she got there all right. I hope Pete met her and everything."

"Well, of course he did," I said, sounding more cheerful than I felt. "And anyway, if he hadn't turned up . . . I mean, let's just say, then Bella would have come straight back here, wouldn't she?"

"Oh, yes," agreed Alice, "of course she would."

The unspoken words "if the forest didn't get her" stayed in the air over our beds and practically glowed like neon lights.

"There's nothing to fear in the forest, Alice, seriously. I know people tell lurid stories and so on, but they're none of them true."

"I know," said Alice, "only sometimes I think that's where Angus must be . . . where he must be living, or something. It's ridiculous, really. I know it is."

"Alice, you are the end," I said. "You are so *irritating* sometimes. Who is Angus? You've never said one word about anyone called Angus before, and I've known you since we were eleven. Are you a dark horse? Or crazy? Or what?"

"I've never told anybody about Angus,

ever," Alice whispered. "I shouldn't have said anything now, either. Forget it, Megan."

"Oh, no I won't," I said. I'd been drifting off to sleep, but I was wide awake now. "You're not getting away with that. Now that you've said this much, you'll have to spill the beans. I do believe you've got a Past, Alice Gregson. Fancy not telling us!"

"There's nothing much to tell," Alice said.

"Don't try and wriggle out of it," I told her. "I want every detail."

"Angus was just a boy. He used to work for us, helping Mr. Foster do the gardening for Dad. He lived in Egerton Parva with his mother. Then my dad sacked him."

"What for?"

There was such a long silence that I had to ask the question again.

"What for, Alice? Come on, let's hear it."

"For trying . . . for trying to kiss me."

"Is that all?"

"He was . . ." Alice was groping for the words. "Rough with me. He . . . he tore my dress a bit. He . . . I don't suppose he meant anything bad, but I couldn't bear him. He used to follow me around and look at me in a horrible way."

"What do you mean, horrible?"

"I can't explain it. As if he was seeing me without my clothes on. I felt . . . all slimy whenever he looked at me, and then he kind of grabbed me one day, to kiss me, and I just screamed and ran away, but he was holding me so tight that a bit of my dress was torn. Oh, Megan, I was terrified! What if he'd touched me with that great slobbery mouth? Oh, I couldn't have borne it . . . and then after my father told him he mustn't come back, not ever, then I felt guilty because I'd made him lose his job."

"It wasn't your fault. If he'd wanted to keep his job he should have behaved himself. He sounds ghastly, like some kind of sex maniac. I think your father was quite right to get rid of him." A thought occurred to me.

"Alice, when was all this?"

"Oh, ages and ages ago. I was thirteen. Nearly thirteen. I don't think of it for months at a time, and then suddenly something happens to remind me . . . like Bella going off in the dark."

"What's Bella got to do with this foul Angus creature?"

"Nothing. Only, sometimes I think he's going to come back for me. I have this nightmare where I'm somewhere dark and he's there, waiting for me. It's horrid."

I laughed, to cheer myself up as much as to comfort Alice, and said, "I don't fancy Angus's chances if Bella gets hold of him! She'll give him such an earful, he'll run away and never be seen again."

I was rewarded by a faint laugh from Alice, and after that we slid into sleep.

It was six o'clock the next morning when Bella tapped on the window.

"Leaving it a bit late, aren't you?" I said. "It's breakfast time in a couple of hours."

"Oh, but Megan, it was so super! Absolutely the best thing ever! A real, proper dance . . . and I was such a hit, honestly. You'll never believe how much everyone loved my songs. And I've danced till my feet are worn down to the ankles. It was blissful. Completely divine. And the food! Look, I've even brought back some lovely little marzipan whad-youmacallits . . . *petits fours* . . . for you and Alice . . . oh, Megan, don't you even want to hear about it?"

"Later, Bella," I groaned. "Later. Please let me sleep now. I'll listen after breakfast."

I tried to get back to sleep, but it was difficult. Bella was singing her favorite song under her breath, but it was loud enough to disturb me . . . something about love and roller coasters and things getting closer and going faster.

Blast Bella and blast Buddy Holly! I pulled my pillow over my head and closed my eyes.

LONDON *April 25, 1962*

Bella came to visit yesterday. She was just up for the day, going to have something done at the dentist's. She asked how we were getting on, and I told her "Fine"—and we are, in a way, aren't we? It was difficult at the beginning, I'm not denying it. It became clear to me during those first days, as I dragged around London from one distressing little apartment to the next while you traveled about looking for work, that love gets very easily pushed to the margins of one's life when it's a question of a roof over your head and the next meal. I'm not saying we ever starved or slept in the street, only that it's easy to have love as your major preoccupation when you have no other urgent problems to think about. It's been much better since we found this room and since you found a job, but, oh, how small and unlovely this place is during the long hours when you're not here! I look at the cracks in the ceiling and the blistering paintwork of the windowsill. I consider the ghosts of flowers in the greasy carpet. I get into the rusty bath, uncomfortably suspicious that I haven't made it properly clean however hard I've scrubbed it. I cook baked beans on our hot plate and we eat on a table branded with the circular marks of other people's cups of coffee. It's hard to feel romantic.

The next time Simon came to the Tower Room, I was still feeling aggrieved about what Fiona had told me. It wasn't so much that I was jealous, as that I resented not being told what a chummy relationship he had with Dorothy. I felt excluded. Simon noticed immediately. Well, it wasn't difficult. Usually, I'd run into his arms the minute he came through the window. On this occasion, though, I sat stiffly on my bed, with my face turned away from him.

"Megan, are you all right?" he asked, coming to sit beside me. "Megan, look at me, please. Why aren't you saying anything?"

"There's nothing to say," I answered in a whisper.

"Oh, come on, Megan! There's obviously something troubling you. Is it something I've said? Something I've done? Do tell me, Megan . . . this is just a waste of time. We have

so little time together. Don't let's quarrel."
He took off the elastic band that held my plait
and shook my hair free.

"I'm not quarreling, as far as I can see."

Simon sighed and stood up. "If you won't
talk to me or tell me what's wrong, then I
might as well leave." He turned toward the
window. I couldn't, simply couldn't bear for
him to leave. I felt as though I were being
slowly torn apart from the inside.

"No, Simon, stay. Please stay. I'll tell you
everything. It's not that I don't want to tell
you, and it's nothing you've done, only it's . . .
it's embarrassing. I shall feel such a fool even
saying it."

"Say it. Go on. Get it over with."

"Very well It's Dorothy. I've never seen
her like that in all the years I've known her.
She . . . she was flirting with you, Simon, at
the tea party. It looked as if she were . . ."

"She's a bit keen on me, it's true," said
Simon, "only Megan, you *must* believe me, it's
nothing I've said or done. Honestly. I'm just
normally friendly, that's all, and she . . . well,
it started with a sort of motherly kind of
thing . . . she'd give me tea, and we'd talk
about my work and so forth, but now I have to
make excuses. I feel funny going to her flat. I

think she's fond of me, and, well, I don't really
know how to behave. I mean, I don't want to
upset her or anything, but I don't want her
getting the wrong idea, either."

"I see. But, Simon, what does she *do*? I can't
imagine it. Has she kissed you?"

"Oh, no, no," Simon frowned. "It's nothing
like that. It's just . . . she comes and sits next to
me if I'm on the sofa and touches my hand if
she gives me a plate—that kind of thing. In the
labs she's always coming in for little chats. It
isn't anything I can't cope with. I just wish you
hadn't seen it."

"I don't mind," I said, "if you promise me,
cross your heart and hope to die, that you're
not keen on Dorothy."

Simon started laughing. "You must surely
be joking! She could be my mother. Oh,
Megan, you are an idiot! Haven't you got the
foggiest idea about what I feel? Am I that
tongue-tied that I haven't made it clear to
you? It's you I love, Megan. You and nobody
else. I don't know how much more plainly I
can say it: listen. I love you."

"Say it again."

"I love you. Love you and love you and love
you."

"Really?"

"Truly."

"And I love you," I said. I had never said the words out loud before. They floated in the darkness of the Tower Room like stars. My mouth felt full of sweetness.

"Don't turn the light on, Megan," Simon whispered. "Come here." So I let him make love to me, and I was glad I did.

Afterward, all alone again, I lay trembling in the dark. I felt as though I were no longer contained within my flesh, but spread out like a piece of shining satin on the bed.

One day a couple of weeks after that night, I came into my study after lunch and found Dorothy sitting in one of the armchairs. She hardly ever came into Austen House.

"Dorothy!" I said. "Has something happened?"

She was looking rather pale, I thought, and all signs of that flirtatious manner I'd caught a glimpse of had disappeared.

"No, dear," she said, "I was simply passing the study on my way to see Miss Herbert and thought I would give you your pocket money for the month. You appear to have forgotten all about it."

"I'm sorry, Dorothy, only I've been so busy, you see."

"Indeed. Well, here's five pounds. Will that be enough until the end of term, do you think?"

"Oh, yes, thank you, Dorothy."

My pocket money, which bought me such things as stamps and stockings and bars of chocolate from the Tuck Shop, came from the same fund as my school fees: the money my parents had left me when they died. There wasn't an enormous amount, but it was enough to allow me to finish my education. Dorothy handed me five one-pound notes and left the room, nodding good-bye rather frostily, I thought. I put my books down on the desk, and it was then that I saw the note. It wasn't even in an envelope, just hastily folded over and put on my desk, but I recognized my name in Simon's writing. My legs suddenly felt very weak, and in the split second before I opened it, I imagined all kinds of dreadful things were going to be contained in it: just as it said in all the magazines I'd read, he'd lost his respect for me, now that we were lovers. He'd had second thoughts. He didn't really love me. This is what it actually said:

My Megan,
What about Sunday? Can you possibly miss
the lecture? If you can, 7:00 P.M.
    I love you.
        Simon.

I was so happy I burst into tears, and when
Bella and Alice came into the study, I was sob-
bing from pure joy. I had meant, honestly and
truly meant, to keep my secret to myself, and I
had been successful for quite a long time, but
now Bella read the note and guessed at once.

"You've done it," she said. "I knew you
would in the end. I told you you'd be the first.
When did it happen?"

"Bella, shut up and don't be coarse. Can't
you see Megan's upset?" said Alice.

"I'm not upset," I sniffed. "I'm radiant with
happiness, can't you tell?"

We all subsided in helpless giggles after
that.

"Was it wonderful? Was it like Saint John
of the Cross?" Bella wanted to know.

"Exactly!" I said. "Like Saint John and
Keats and everybody else."

"And Buddy Holly?" Bella continued.

"Naturally. And Elvis and Racine and
Shakespeare, oh, everybody you can think of!"

"Are you going to tell us what it was like? I'm dying to know every detail."

"Bella, you're disgusting." Alice shivered delicately. "How can you be so matter-of-fact about it? I don't understand you."

"It's a very matter-of-fact event, Alice, and in case it's escaped your notice, it's going on all over the place all the time. It's what's responsible for human life on the planet, no less, so you'd better stop being so prissy and stuck-up about it. It's not an awesome mystery, it's a fact of life!" Bella's cheeks were flushed with passion.

Alice was unrepentant. "I don't care if it *is* a fact of life. It's private. You've got no right to go poking and prying all over the place. Fancy asking when it happened! It's none of your business."

"Stop it!" I said. "Just stop fighting, that's all. I won't tell you anything I don't want to tell you. It isn't worth quarreling about, honestly."

"Then we won't," said Bella promptly. If she was quick to lose her temper, she was even quicker at forgetting all about it. She grinned at Alice. "We'll be the best of friends."

Peace was restored and eventually the

conversation strayed away from my love life
and on to other things.

Lectures at Egerton Hall were supposed to be
special treats. All kinds of interesting people
came to talk to us about every subject under
the sun. There were Geographical lectures
(Up the Amazon with Notebook and Cam-
era), Careers lectures (My Days as a Junior
Policewoman), Cultural lectures (Poets I Remember, by a Famous Publisher), and sometimes lectures turned into recitals, and the
grand piano would be played by ladies with
dancing fingers, or we would be sung at by
plump tenors who were never anywhere near
handsome enough. Some of the lectures were
interesting, some were entertaining, and
others were dreadfully boring, but you could
always daydream if the worst came to the
worst while the long, wooden pointer stabbed
at the white canvas screen and the color slides
clicked into place, sometimes upside down. It
was quite easy to miss a lecture if you were in
the Sixth Form. You simply had to ask Miss
Herbert.

"It's not like you, Megan dear . . . you're
usually interested in everything. Still, if you
feel you *must* work . . . but would you still see

everyone into the Hall quietly for me? I'd be so grateful."

"Yes, of course," I said, but my heart jumped in alarm. It would be at least ten past seven by the time everyone was sitting quietly and the lecture had started. Would Simon wait for me? I had no way of telling him. I would have to be patient and hope. I stood at the bottom of the steps leading to the Hall, assuming that everyone was behaving themselves and marching in fairly quietly. They could have done the Conga or a tap dance up the stairs for all the attention they were getting from me. I was somewhere else. I was with Simon, climbing the scaffolding, looking up and up toward the lighted window of the Tower Room. I was already, in my own mind, making my way up the stairs, past Matron's room and Miss Herbert's room and into his arms. Oh, if only he would wait for me! Surely he must? As the doors of the Hall closed, I looked at my watch. 7:15 exactly. I flew down School Corridor and along Study Passage and up the stairs, silently praying that I wouldn't bump into anyone, that I wouldn't have to stop. Austen House was quiet. Perhaps Simon and I would be the only ones stirring. I reached the Tower Room and opened the door. Simon was standing near the window and beside him, in front of the chest of drawers, was Dorothy.

"Ah, Megan," she said in a voice like steel wool. "We have been waiting for you. Come and sit down."

I wanted to turn around and run away. I wanted cracks in the floorboards to open and let me through, out of reach of Dorothy's pale eyes, but I went into the Tower Room. What else could I have done? I looked at Simon, but he wouldn't meet my eyes. Dorothy spoke in a flat, even tone that nevertheless managed to sound . . . what? Disgusted? Angry? Hurt? Perhaps a little of all of those. She said:

"You will doubtless be wondering, Megan, how it is that I am here, in your"—she paused—"love nest." I could hear the quotation marks in her voice as she said that. The phrase reminded me of sordid stories in the *News of the World*, which, of course, was Dorothy's intention. "If you will leave notes to Megan half open on her desk, Simon, then you must not be surprised if people read them, must you?"

Simon stood up straight and looked at Dorothy. "I don't mind who reads my notes," he said bravely. "I have nothing to hide. The fact is, I love Megan."

It was as if those three words had ignited something in Dorothy. Suddenly, she began to shriek at us, every feeling she had ever had that had lain concealed for so long rising and bubbling out of her lips like burning lava from the center of a volcano.

"Facts! You dare to talk to me about facts! I'll tell you some facts, if that's what you enjoy. Fact One: You no more know what love is than two pigs wallowing in your own filth. All that kissing and pawing and yes, far, far worse, I've no doubt, has got nothing to do with love. Fact Two: You have been dishonest, both of you. Deceitful and underhanded and wicked, creeping up here for your disgusting little sordid pleasures when other people are going about their normal lives. This is a school, Megan, not a brothel. Bedrooms are out of bounds to visitors, did you know that? And how dare you betray *me*? After all these years ... all I've done for you. What would your parents say if they could see you crawling upstairs to meet this ... this ..." She burst into tears then and fell weeping onto Bella's bed. I didn't know what to do, what to say. I had never seen Dorothy like this. She seemed to be disintegrating, unraveling before my eyes.

"Dorothy," I said finally. "I couldn't help it.

I wanted to, but I couldn't. I love Simon. We love one another."

"And me?" Dorothy said. "What about me? What about what I feel?"

"Oh, Dorothy," I said, thinking that she felt somehow that I'd rejected her, that I no longer loved her. "I'm sorry. Of course I love you, too, and wouldn't hurt you for anything."

But she wasn't even looking at me. She was staring at Simon, tears streaming out of her eyes, and her mouth all twisted up. She stood up and walked over to him. He backed up against the window, but she kept getting nearer and nearer to him, until she was standing right up next to him, pressing her body against his. He flinched backward, but Dorothy was now out of control. I watched, frozen with terror, as she beat against his chest with her hands fixed into claws.

"Didn't I mean anything? Didn't you care, not even a bit? All my help ... why do you think I brought you here? Simon, Simon, answer me ..." She moaned and writhed against him, and then brought her hands to his face. His glasses flew on to the floor and Dorothy turned and stamped on them with the solid heel of her shoe. She stamped and stamped until the lenses were ground to dust on the Tower Room floor. Then she slumped onto Bella's bed again, as though the destruction of Simon's glasses had exhausted her.

"Dorothy, listen," said Simon. "Megan and I are both very fond of you. This . . . this isn't like you. Shall I take you back to your room and make you some tea?"

Dorothy looked up at him. Then she visibly pulled herself together. By the time she spoke, some of the steel was back in her voice.

"I wish to have nothing more to do with either of you. You have betrayed me. Simon Findlay, you are dismissed. I shall write you a check for any money the school owes you. And not only that, I have to warn you that a carefully worded letter will be on its way to your next employers tomorrow. I think," she smiled, "you will have to set about finding yourself another position. You must leave Egerton Hall tonight, both of you."

"We have nowhere to go," said Simon.

"I can't help that," said Dorothy. "Megan, go to my flat and bring a suitcase. I want you packed and out of school before the end of tonight's lecture."

"But Bella and Alice are in there!" I said. "Can't I wait and just say good-bye to them?"

"Certainly not," said Dorothy. "I shall inform them. I shall also inform Miss Herbert."

"Can I . . . will you give me some money?"

Dorothy laughed. "Your parents' money," she said, "is put away for you until your twenty-first birthday, as you know very well. It is, until then, to be used for your education."

"I have enough money for us both," said Simon. "Come on, Megan, let's go and pack."

I followed him out of the room, leaving Dorothy there alone. I wanted to say so many things, wanted to try and explain so much, but the words wouldn't come out, and whatever I did, I couldn't bring myself to look at Dorothy. In a darkened Study Passage, Simon said, "I'll meet you in front of Main School. It won't take me more than half an hour to pack."

"Oh, Simon," I cried. "What will happen to us? What will we do?"

"We," he said, "will live happily ever after. But first, we'll drive to London and find somewhere to live."

"How can you drive? She smashed your glasses." I put my hand out and stroked his face. In her heart, I thought, she wanted to blind him. I stood on tiptoe and kissed his closed eyes, and we clung together for a moment, trembling.

"I've got," he murmured, "a spare pair."

I hadn't realized until I started packing that night how very little I owned. A few clothes and a few books, that's all. I left my uniform behind and filled up the space in the suitcase with textbooks and exercise books full of my essays. I hid a note to Alice and Bella in Alice's nightdress case. It said:

> Can't write more than this. Dorothy found out about S. and me. S. has been sacked, and I think I've been expelled. In any case, we're leaving. Don't know where we're going. I'll write and tell you my address.
> Megan
> P.S. She wouldn't let me stay and say good-bye.

There was no one about at all as we drove away from Egerton Hall. A thin, sleety rain was falling, blowing against the windshield in a flurry of drops like tears. The last verse of "The Eve of St. Agnes" came into my head:

> And they are gone: aye, ages long ago
> These lovers fled away into the storm.

I sat in the front seat of Simon's car, and Egerton Hall shrank into the darkness as we went down the drive toward the forest and what lay beyond.

LONDON *April 30, 1962*

Simon, I love you. I don't want you to think there's any doubt about that. I love you and I always will, probably, but what worries me is this: I want more. Is that greedy? I don't mean more of your love, or more of you, not really, because I know you have to work and be away all day, and I know (I think I know) that you love me, but I want . . . what? My friends, my lessons, to take my A-levels and go to university. I want to travel and go to parties and meet lots of different people, do all kinds of things and above all, be able to go back to Egerton Hall. That may sound strange to you, but you have to remember it's my home, the only one I've known since I was eleven. Also, I would like to make my peace with Dorothy. All this time I have been worrying: What will she say to me? How will she react when I return? The dread I've felt about this has nearly been enough to stop me from going back, but I must. I have to face Dorothy. I have to listen to whatever she says, and answer it. How, I have no idea, but I must. I know her shortcomings, but still she is my guardian and has done her best for me all this time. I want to visit Miss van der Leyden in the hospital. I want to go to Alice's birthday party in June. I know what you'll say: why can't I do all those things and still stay with you? The answer is: there isn't enough money if I don't work, so I have to spend my days in that dreadful coffee shop, and then where does all the time go? I can't study, or read, or see my friends. All I'm capable of when I'm not working is writing this. And doesn't our love outweigh all this? I don't know, Simon, truly. I don't know. Sometimes I feel I've spent years and years in one room at the top of a winding flight of stairs, looking out of the window at life, instead of taking part in it like everybody else. And I get the letters, Simon, all those siren voices saying, "Come back, come back to us!" From Bella, Alice, Miss Herbert, Miss Clarke ... everyone has written except Dorothy. And even Dorothy, if I returned ... if I could explain, there is a chance that she would speak to me again now after all this time. I can't say I love her as one should love a mother, but she is still responsible for me, and I, for my part, feel nothing but sorrow for her, understanding how much she must have wanted you. She is, in that respect, no different from me, so how could I hate her?

I can't think what my future will be if I stay,

Simon, and that's the truth. Sometimes I feel that you don't love me in the same way I've loved you. In my darkest moods I think you simply followed your inclinations and desires: did whatever you wanted to, both with Dorothy and with me, but I know that's not fair. Everything you wanted I wanted even more. If I go back, we can write to one another, see each other in the holidays. There's no need to part, not really. Not forever. If our love is real, and I think it is, then it ought to survive. And from your point of view, Simon, if you are without me to look after, you can go anywhere, get any sort of job at all. Admit that that's a very tempting prospect.

I hope you read this, my dear love, by the time I return. I have made an appointment with Armand, Bella's hairdresser. He is going to cut my hair. I know you will be angry with me. I know how much you love it. Sometimes it's seemed to me as though you want to splash in it as if it were liquid, cover yourself with it, drown in it, almost as though it were separate from me. I shall miss your hands on it and through it and in it, and how your face buried in it makes me feel. But whenever it's done up in a plait, which it is most of the time, I think of it as a rope that's hung down my back for years, tying me together, tying me down, tying me to Dorothy and my childhood. Soon, it will be gone. I will return to Egerton Hall with hair as short as any boy's. Bella will think me fashionable at last, but I will know that what I am is free.